## THE MISTLETOE TEST
by Diane Farr

*A Regency Romance*

**Other books by this author:**

The Nobody

Playing to Win (*originally published as* Fair Game)

Falling for Chloe

Once Upon A Christmas

Dashing Through the Snow (*originally published as* Reckless Miss Ripley *in the anthology* A Regency Christmas Eve)

The Fortune Hunter

Duel of Hearts

Under the Wishing Star

Under A Lucky Star

Wicked Cool

Scary Cool

Epic Cool

information is available at dianefarrbooks.com

To the San Francisco Giants

Who, despite having a terrible year,

distracted my husband

and enabled me to finish this book

**ACKNOWLEDGMENTS**

The author extends her heartfelt thanks to Anna Riggs, Archivist at the Bath Abbey, for her invaluable research assistance, to Suz DeMello for her encouragement and editorial expertise, and to Mary Beth Barber for knowing more about Microsoft Word than Microsoft does.

# Chapter One

*Bath*
*November, 1822*

Felicity Pennington rapped briskly on her godmother's library door and opened it, not waiting for a response.

Lady DuFrayne was propped on a fainting couch amid a welter of pillows. She glared balefully at her goddaughter. "I didn't say 'come in,'" she snapped. "Where the devil is Murdock?"

Felicity paused on the threshold. She raised an eyebrow and returned stare for stare.

Her ladyship scowled. "Very well," she grumbled. "Come in."

Felicity came in, closing the door behind her. "Really, Aunt Agnes, your language is deplorable. I told Murdock I would announce myself, as usual. Since you are well enough to receive me in the library—"

"Don't be impertinent. Is that a new hat? The crown's too high. You look like a beanpole with a basket on top."

"I like it." Felicity crossed the room with her light, firm tread and bent to kiss her aunt's delicately-perfumed cheek. It reassured her to perceive the powder and scent; Aunt Agnes was hardly at death's door. Even so, it was a bit jarring to see haughty Lady DuFrayne, the terror of the Pump Room, reduced to her present state. Her slippered feet were up, her lap was covered with a shawl, and a small table had been set near her left hand. It bore a jumble of vials and pill boxes, a carafe of water, a tumbler, a half-drunk cup of tea sitting crookedly in a saucer, three spoons, a bell, and a stack of handkerchiefs. Aunt Agnes, poor dear, looked cross and uncomfortable.

"How are you feeling?"

Aunt Agnes pointed to the overloaded table, her lips thinning in disgust. "The answer is obvious, is it not? I feel terrible."

"I feared as much," exclaimed Felicity. "Murdock is quite right, for once. You should not have come downstairs."

"I don't take medical advice from my butler," said Aunt Agnes testily. "If I must cough myself to death, I'd rather do it sitting upright than lying on that dratted bed." She waved Felicity to a chair. "Don't make me crane my neck, child. Sit down."

Felicity obediently sat, casting a practiced eye over her aunt's sharp features. She looked even more out of sorts than usual, but beneath the cosmetics her color seemed good. "Dr. Fillmore tells us you are in no danger."Aunt Agnes gave a derisive snort, then coughed. "Dr. Fillmore is a heartless quack." She thumped her pillows bitterly. "I've half a mind to throw all his physics in the fire. If I did, however, I daresay the place would go up like a torch. That stuff in the green vial is gin."

"Oh, surely not—"

"Gin!" barked Aunt Agnes. "Nothing more than gin—and not the best gin! Fillmore thought I wouldn't recognize the taste. Ha! I wasn't born yesterday." She looked like an enraged falcon, ruffled feathers and all. "I hope to high heaven you have come here to amuse me. I am excessively bored."

"Well, not to amuse you, exactly. But perhaps I can distract you a bit."

"That's nearly as good."

"Indeed, ma'am, I hope you will still think so when you hear what I have come to say."

An arrested look crossed Lady DuFrayne's aquiline features. Her hawk-like eyes gleamed beneath her finely-arched brows. "I see what it is," she said, with grim relish. "You've come to tell me something I shan't like to hear."

Felicity bit her lip. "Not quite," she temporized. "That is—*I* find it unpleasant, but there is no reason for you to view it in the same light."

"I'll be the judge of that. What is it?"

Felicity almost laughed aloud. Aunt Agnes looked better already.

"Two things, really." She held up a finger. "One, I don't think you should take me to London in the spring."

Lady DuFrayne pulled herself upright, swelling with outrage. Before she could speak, Felicity held up a second finger. "Two, I think you should take Lulu instead."

"*Lulu?*"

Shock wiped Aunt Agnes's face completely blank, then sent her into a coughing fit. The shock must have been severe, for the coughing fit was violent. Felicity, filled with remorse, flew to the little table and pawed through the medicines, seeking something to quiet her aunt's paroxysm. Aunt Agnes waved feebly at her, still coughing.

Felicity withdrew to a respectful distance and observed. "I see by your gestures that you wish me to leave. But I shan't go home, if that's what you are trying to pantomime. Not until I see you breathing normally."

Aunt Agnes glared. "I shall never," she wheezed, "breathe normally again. Could have sworn ... you said ... take Lulu to London." She picked up her cold tea with a shaking hand and took a gulp.

"That is precisely what I said."

The teacup clattered back into the saucer. Aunt Agnes fell back upon her pillows, apparently speechless.

Felicity crossed back to her and sat, taking her aunt's unresponsive hand in an affectionate clasp. "Dear Aunt Agnes," she said softly. "You have always been so kind to me. So generous."

Aunt Agnes scowled. "Rubbish," she said weakly. "Goddaughter."

"I know I am your goddaughter, but you have been kinder to me than any godmother need be. You have given me not one, but *five* Seasons in London. If you take me again this coming year, that will be six. You must own, six Seasons is excessive. We both know what the purpose of a London Season is: to contract a suitable marriage. But no gentleman has shown the slightest interest in me in all this time."

Aunt Agnes looked a bit startled behind her scowl. It seemed she had not bothered to count the years as they went by. "A sixth Season. I had not realized ... how old are you, my dear?"

"Three and twenty. I shall turn twenty-four in May."

Lady DuFrayne's frown cleared. "Pooh! And it's not yet December. You're a child."

"I am *not* a child, and it is a waste of your money to trot me out, year after year, with no results. It is high time I stepped aside. Pray recall that I have three younger sisters. How long must they wait for their chance, while you dangle me before the *ton* like an unwanted carrot?"

Aunt Agnes plucked at the edge of the shawl with restless fingers. "What's the matter with the men, these days?" she grumbled. "They must all be nincompoops. A female of your caliber should have received a dozen offers by now." Her eyes gleamed. "One day, Felicity, you will find a man who is not a nincompoop. Mark my words."

Felicity bit back a laugh. She did not ascribe her unmarried state to the idiocy of modern men. A mere Miss Pennington from Bath, with few connections and no fortune, must be exceptionally appealing to rise to the attention of the *ton*. She saw little point in contradicting Aunt Agnes, however. "I hope you are right, of course," she said placidly. "But while we are waiting, I think you should take Lulu to London in my place."

Aunt Agnes looked askance at her. "You can't be serious."

"I am perfectly serious. Lulu is nineteen now, you know."

"Well, she doesn't act it," said Aunt Agnes with asperity. "Does she still bounce about the room like a rubber ball?"

"No, no," said Felicity earnestly. "I assure you, she has overcome that tendency almost completely. Nowadays, she often sits still—or nearly still—for several minutes at a time."

Aunt Agnes shuddered. "The last time she was here, she threw a vase at the wall. Sèvres porcelain! Irreplaceable."

"Now, Aunt Agnes, you know that is unjust. It was purely an accident. Lulu brushed it with the edge of her skirt and knocked it to the floor; the sort of thing that might happen to anyone."

"Had she not been *bouncing*—"

"And you have, in fact, replaced it," Felicity

added hastily, with a bright, determined smile. "All's well that ends well."

"Felicity, do not argue with me. Lulu is a walking thunderplump. And besides, she's not my goddaughter. I owe her no particular duty. I refuse to set her loose in London—or, indeed, any city that contains breakable objects."

"I would never argue with you, Aunt Agnes," Felicity assured her mendaciously. "I am merely appealing to your sense of justice. I know your sense of justice is keen."

"It is outweighed, however, by my sense of self-preservation," Lady DuFrayne retorted. "It is bad enough that you propose to abandon me. But to foist that Lulu on me in your stead—no! I'm an old woman. I'd never survive it."

This was too much. Felicity stiffened. "You needn't refer to her as *that Lulu*. There is nothing wrong with Lulu. She's a sweet, loving, wonderful girl. She's merely a trifle..." She searched for the word. "Eager."

"Eager!"

"Exuberant," amended Felicity. "She has a great deal of ... of verve. It's charming! Those of us who know her well, love her very much."

Aunt Agnes looked exasperated. "Felicity, I haven't the stamina to spend three months in London with Lulu's *verve*. And I would find her conversation as exhausting as her company, I daresay! I can't abide hen-witted females."

"She only appears foolish around you, Aunt Agnes. You make her nervous." Felicity looked severely at her godmother. "You can scarcely blame her for that. You know perfectly well that you have that effect on most people."

Aunt Agnes's lips twitched, and she gave a deep chuckle. The laughter, unfortunately, sent her into another coughing spell. Felicity seized the opportunity to press her point. "Lulu isn't hen-witted. She's clever and funny. I am persuaded that when the two of you know each other better, you will become great friends."

"Both of us ... already ... great friends with you. You come, too."

Felicity opened her mouth to protest, but Aunt Agnes held up an imperious hand, commanding her to silence while she struggled to stop coughing. "I shall give ... that Lulu ... a Season ... on one condition." She took a careful breath. "You must come along, Felicity. You can be a ... buffer ... between the two of us."

"But the expense! My dear Aunt Agnes, the entire point of my proposal is to spare you the expense of—"

"Stop. Not one more word." Aunt Agnes's voice was weak at the moment, but she still knew how to command. Felicity fell silent. Aunt Agnes glared at her, one hand pressed to her chest as if holding back the coughs by force. "Presumptuous chit. Do you think I care for the expense? I am not a nipfarthing. It's my own convenience I care for." Her breath wheezed in and out. "'Twill go more smoothly if you come along. You may shepherd that dratted pea-goose about. Spare me the trouble. I'm not as young as I once was."

Felicity tapped her foot, irresolute. Aunt Agnes was not alone in wishing for Felicity's company during the trip. Lulu was panting to go to London, but her enthusiasm had definitely dimmed when it became clear that Felicity intended to stay behind. "Very well," she said at last. And then she could not hold back her smile as a bubble of relief rose in her. "Thank you, Aunt Agnes. I know I should not accept such a shocking degree of generosity, but I am too selfish to pretend I actually *want* to stay home. I did try to be noble."

"Duly noted." Aunt Agnes's eyes gleamed

with wry humor.

"I'm afraid I have another favor to ask of you." Felicity hesitated. Her smile turned rueful. "I had pictured asking this, you know, after explaining to you how much money would be saved by my not going to London."

"Hmpf. Then you've an *expensive* favor to ask of me."

"Well, yes," said Felicity apologetically. "Because, as you yourself have remarked, Lulu would benefit from acquiring a few social graces. Preferably before her London debut—not after."

Aunt Agnes shot her a darkling glance and muttered something impolite about silk purses and sow's ears. Felicity pretended not to hear. "I was thinking we could bring her out, in a small way, in Bath. Just to give her a little confidence, you know."

"When?"

"Now. This winter. I would do most of the work, of course. But I need you to host a party. A very small party," she added anxiously, as Aunt Agnes's expression grew more and more hostile. "Just a few, hand-picked people, so that Lulu may make her debut among friends."

"Ha! Although you will not say so, you plainly agree with me that Lulu is hopeless. That is why you are urging me to take extra pains on her behalf." Aunt Agnes's mouth set in grim lines. "Well, I will do it."

Felicity almost jumped with surprise. Aunt Agnes waved away her stammered gratitude, bending a keen, unsmiling gaze upon her goddaughter. "I have a great fondness for you, Felicity," she said dryly. "And I do feel an obligation to your mother and sisters as well. But I hope you realize that *you* are the cream of the crop. If you have found it difficult to attract a husband, Lulu will find it impossible."

14

Felicity snatched up her aunt's frail hand and kissed it before she could pull it away. "You talk a great deal of nonsense, Aunt, but you are the soul of generosity."

"Poppycock. I please myself, as always." But her lips twitched as she suppressed a smile. "You approached me in a moment of weakness. You might have received a different answer, had I not been suffering from ennui. But as long as you take on the project while I stay safely out of the way, watching Lulu gallop through the Polite World might be vastly entertaining."

Felicity laughed. "True, but I think you are underestimating Lulu. She may do very well. There is a sweetness about her, a certain something that cries out for masculine protection—a quality that I, lamentably, lack."

"Oh, she cries out for protection; I'll grant you that," said Aunt Agnes acidly. "I cry out for protection, myself, when Lulu enters the room."

The wind had picked up by the time Lady DuFrayne's elegant front door closed behind Felicity. She hesitated on the stoop, one hand firmly on her hat as the wind tugged at it. A mud-spattered coach was rounding the corner, piled high with baggage and precariously swaying. Her instinct was to let it pass before stepping onto the pavement, but to her surprise, the coach slowed and stopped directly in front of her, the horses blowing and stamping. She watched with interest as the driver clambered down and opened the passenger door. Whoever was arriving had evidently come from a distance; odd that Aunt Agnes had said nothing to her about expecting visitors. It seemed likely that the driver had mistaken his destination.

This opinion became conviction when she saw the coach's occupant. A gentleman emerged. He was a young man, tall, with something indefinably rakish about him. And he was clearly a foreigner. Aunt Agnes disapproved of foreigners. His clothing was expensive, well-cut and flattering, but not in the first stare of fashion, and his complexion was as swarthy as a sailor's. No Englishman – certainly no English gentleman – could have burnt himself so brown. Between the tanned skin and the rakish air, Felicity was irresistibly reminded of pirates from days of old. This man would look perfectly at home in an open-throated shirt with sea-boots on his feet and a cutlass in his hand.

He paused when he saw her, meeting her gaze with piercing, dark eyes. Felicity was annoyed to sense a strong frisson of attraction, which she sternly repressed even as one of the man's eyebrows shot up. He said nothing, however, but turned to finish paying off the driver.

"I beg your pardon," said Felicity politely. "But I think you may have come to the wrong address."

"Do you?" said the man, not bothering to look up. "I don't."

She decided to overlook his rudeness; one must give foreigners the benefit of the doubt. Perhaps, in his culture, contradicting a helpful stranger was not a breach of decorum. "I suppose it is no concern of mine—" she began, but the gentleman, having paid off the driver, looked up at her again. His grin stopped her in mid-sentence.

"I didn't say it was no concern of yours," he told her. "I only said you were wrong."

Felicity's world turned on its axis as a

shock of recognition hit her. "Gavin!" she gasped, her mind reeling. "Merciful heavens – is it you?"

He laughed and mounted the steps to shake her hand. "It is. Am I so altered that my own cousin does not recognize me?"

"Yes," she said frankly. "Although I am not your cousin, as well you know. How do you do? You look like a pirate."

He laughed. Felicity, looking at him with new eyes, thought that the changes became him. His shoulders seemed wider, his legs, always shapely, were now so well-muscled that she had to avert her gaze quickly to keep from blushing at the sight. Even his sun-darkened skin—while dreadfully uncouth, of course—somehow looked well on him. It would never do to betray any of this, but still … there was no denying that Gavin looked disquietingly handsome. She had never before understood the attraction that London's swooning ladies seemed to feel for her maddening, scapegrace quasi-cousin, Gavin DuFrayne. Now, although far from catching the fever herself, she suddenly thought she understood it.

"I'd have known you anywhere," said Gavin. His gaze swept her, and his grin widened. "Although you've changed, too, during the past five years."

"How unhandsome of you to say so," remarked Felicity. "Island life hasn't improved your manners one whit."

Another bark of laughter escaped him. "I meant it as a compliment, but I daresay you won't believe that. You've always had an air about you, Cousin, but the last time I saw you, you were still a green girl. Town-bronze suits you."

She tilted her chin and regarded him dubiously. It was extremely unlike Gavin to compliment her. On the other hand, she was probably ascribing to him character traits he had long since outgrown. They had been playmates as children, and had bickered and laughed together a great deal in their teens, but she really hadn't spent more than fifteen minutes at a time in his company since then. Once he'd moved to London he'd become quite the man-about-town and they had, naturally, grown apart.

"Town-bronze," she repeated. "It sounds hideous, as if I needed frequent dusting."

"On the contrary. It means you've acquired polish." He reached out one arm and rapped smartly on Aunt Agnes's door. "That's a very dashing bonnet."

"It's a hat," she corrected him, her eyes twinkling. "Bonnet, indeed! You've been away too long."

"There, you see? You've proved my point. Felicity Pennington, setting Gavin DuFrayne straight on a matter of fashion!" He shook his head with mock sorrow. "I never thought I'd see the day."

"Well, you've plenty of time before the Season starts. If you apply yourself, I daresay you'll reach my heights by then."

Murdock opened the door, betraying a flicker of surprise at seeing Felicity still standing where he last saw her. He took Mr. DuFrayne's arrival in stride, however, which made Felicity suspect that Aunt Agnes had known perfectly well that Gavin was coming and had deliberately kept the news from her goddaughter. She mulled this over as she headed home, walking briskly through the chilly afternoon. What did Aunt Agnes's silence portend?

By the time she reached home, her mouth was set in a grim line. Felicity adored her Aunt Agnes but was not blind to her faults. She was a crafty old bird, and fond of setting those around her in a tizzy. She was fully capable of pitting her goddaughter against her nephew, watching the fireworks, and enjoying the show.

It was not the first time Felicity had reflected on the evils of her situation. It had long chafed her to hang on Aunt Agnes's sleeve. Her family was utterly dependent on the DuFrayne fortune—a fortune to which the Penningtons had absolutely no claim, until Agnes Pennington married it. Agnes's fondness for her baby brother had—fortunately for his widow and daughters—extended to his heirs, and when Sir Jasper DuFrayne left the bulk of his fortune to his wife, rather than tie it to the estate as the DuFrayne baronets had always done, Agnes removed to Bath and bought two houses: a large one in Laura Place for herself, and a small one on Henrietta Street for her brother's family.

Felicity would never know which of Aunt Agnes's motivations was stronger: her affection for Mama and the girls, or the delight she took in annoying the DuFraynes. The result was the same, either way. The Penningtons lived on tenterhooks, acutely aware of the necessity of remaining in Aunt Agnes's good graces, and the familial ties they had once enjoyed with the DuFraynes were at an end. There were no more summers or Christmases at Ashwood, the manor house in Kent. Felicity missed those times, and missed the DuFraynes as well, but it could not be helped. With Papa gone, and Mama left with four daughters on her hands and no son to support them, the whims of Lady DuFrayne were all that stood between the Penningtons and poverty.

Her thoughts must have lent her features a sober expression, for as she approached the Penningtons' narrow house she saw Lulu's face— all but pressed against the glass in the drawing room window—fall almost ludicrously from anxiety to despair.

"Oh dear," murmured Felicity, having an idea of what would surely follow. Sure enough, Lulu's face instantly disappeared from the window and Lulu herself hurtled through the front door and clutched Felicity's arm before she could reach the step.

"Is it very bad?" asked Lulu breathlessly. "Is she angry?"

Felicity tried in vain to detach Lulu's fingers from her sleeve. "No, dearest, of course not. Pray do not crease my redingote. All is well. Where is your hat?"

"I don't need a hat. I'm not *going* anywhere."

"If you are not going anywhere, Lulu, let us return to the house rather than converse on the pavement." Since Lulu was still clinging anxiously to Felicity, she was able to draw her sister into the house simply by stepping over the threshold. She closed the door firmly behind them.

"But what did Aunt Agnes say, Felicity? You look frightfully grim." Lulu's enormous blue eyes searched her sister's face. "Or you did, a moment ago."

Their mother's plump form appeared in the drawing room doorway. She looked nearly as anxious as Lulu. Behind Mama peeped Nora's curious face, and the sudden silence from the pianoforte betrayed the fact that even Helena, normally aloof and scornful of social ambitions, felt interested in the outcome of Felicity's conversation with Aunt Agnes.

"Well," remarked Felicity, "I had intended to remove my hat and gloves like a civilized creature before making my announcement, but I see now that I must alter my priorities."

"Indeed you must," said Mrs. Pennington firmly, standing aside to allow her eldest daughter to enter the family's cramped sitting room.

Felicity walked to the hearth rug and began pulling off her gloves as the family settled themselves in their usual spots—Helena at the piano, Mama in her overstuffed chair, Nora and Lulu side-by-side on the sofa. "Well, I shall not keep you in suspense. Aunt Agnes has agreed to take both Lulu and me to London in the spring."

Amid the exclamations of relief and joy, Lulu emitted a sound resembling that of a teakettle coming on to boil. She leapt from the sofa and jumped up and down, hugging herself. Nora, adept from long practice, caught the thimble Lulu knocked off the side table before it could disappear into the sofa cushions. Lulu rushed to Felicity and caught her in a convulsive hug, then dashed to Mama and each of her other sisters in turn, exclaiming, "Oh! Oh! Oh!"

Felicity laid her gloves on the mantel, laughing. "There is more," she said.

"Hush, Lulu, pray," their mother urged, vainly attempting to catch Lulu as she whirled jubilantly round the room.

Felicity raised her voice slightly, to be heard above the commotion. "Aunt Agnes has agreed to bring Lulu out in Bath prior to the Season—immediately, in fact—so we have a little work ahead of us, preparing for a winter debut."

Lulu ceased dashing from spot to spot and resumed jumping up and down. Then she halted, cocking her head like a puzzled puppy. "But Felicity, I already know everyone in Bath."

Felicity paused in the act of removing her hat. "Do you? You astonish me."

"Well, not everyone, of course," Lulu said. "But everyone you would care to have me know. Don't I?"

Mama patted Lulu's hand. "Our friends

think of you as a child, dear one," she said. "With a debut, you will cross the threshold into womanhood."

Felicity checked her reflection in the mantelpiece mirror and tucked a stray lock of hair back into place. "By the time we are done, none of our acquaintance will think of you merely as Lulu. We shall introduce them to Miss Lucille Pennington—with as much fanfare as we can muster."

Lulu stood uncharacteristically still for a moment. Felicity could not tell if the prospect of becoming Miss Lucille Pennington was dazzling Lulu or terrifying her. She offered her younger sister an encouraging smile. "It will be great fun, Lulu, I promise you. And there is still more."

Nora's face lit with hope. "Am I to go to London too?"

Felicity burst out laughing. "No, nothing as wonderful as that. But as you are only sixteen, do not despair! Your turn will surely come."

Lulu's animation returned. "I will sponsor Nora!" she exclaimed. "For once I am married, we need no longer depend on Aunt Agnes for everything."

Helena's deep chuckle cut through the general outcry that met this announcement. "Lulu, you *are* an optimist," she remarked.

"Why shouldn't I be?" demanded Lulu, visibly hurt by her family's seemingly-low expectations for her. "It's the whole point of my going. Isn't it?"

"Well, yes," said Felicity. "But it's best to approach the matter one step at a time. First a new wardrobe, then dancing lessons, then a few introductions, then a brilliant marriage, *then* Nora's presentation. I never made it past step three—"

"You said you had more news," Mama

reminded her.

"Ah. Yes." Felicity hesitated. She had a feeling this bit of news would not be met with jubilation. "Gavin DuFrayne has returned from the West Indies."

"Oh dear," said Mama faintly. Her blue eyes went wide with apprehension. "Permanently?"

"I did not think to ask him."

"What! You spoke with him?"

"Yes, Mama. He is visiting Aunt Agnes."

Mama twisted her handkerchief in her lap. "Oh dear," she said again. "How unfortunate, to be sure. Well, we must hope his visit is not a long one. Was he rude to you?"

Felicity laughed. "No more than he ever was. I do not regard it."

Mama sighed. "He will do his best to distance your aunt from us, mark my words. All the DuFraynes resent us. I shudder to think what he'll say when he learns that Agnes means to bring Lulu out."

Felicity waved an airy hand. "Pooh. He may say whatever he likes; Aunt Agnes will pay no heed. She never listens to anyone once she has set her mind on something."

Mama did not appear convinced. "Well, you know her best, of course. I hope you are right. Lulu will be so disappointed if—"

"If nothing," said Felicity firmly. "We have no reason to believe that Gavin shares his family's attitude toward us. And if he does, I am more than a match for Gavin DuFrayne, mark my words."

## Chapter Two

Meanwhile, in Aunt Agnes's spacious marble hall, Gavin DuFrayne was grinding his teeth. He had known he would encounter Felicity Pennington in Bath, but to see her standing on Aunt Agnes's doorstep, as bold as brass—and dressed to the nines—had ruffled his temper. Felicity had never been a beauty, but she carried herself with supreme confidence, and from the top of her absurdly-tall hat to the tips of her stylish kid half-boots she looked every inch the lady of fashion.

He begrudged her every button and feather. That, he had expected. What he had not expected was that he'd be glad to see her.

Glad to see her! He cursed himself for a sentimental fool. He'd stupidly forgotten how much he liked her. Felicity Pennington had always been a breath of fresh air, and now that bracing blast carried with it a thousand pleasant boyhood memories. The instant he saw her familiar face, alight with the intelligence and good humor he'd once been so fond of, the years seemed to fall away.

But a wave of nostalgia would not alter his plans one whit. He'd come here to thrust a spoke in the Penningtons' wheel, and misplaced sentiment would not deter him. He had a duty to his family, and meant to detach the Pennington leeches presently draining the DuFrayne fortune.

Murdock's gloomy face appeared at the library door. "She will see you now, Mr. DuFrayne."

"It's Sir Gavin now. But never mind." He strolled past Murdock before the butler could correct himself. Aunt Agnes was wrapped up and propped on a settee like an invalid, but what afflicted her appeared to be nothing worse than la grippe. "How do you do, Aunt?"

"Poorly," she snapped. "But if you're anticipating my imminent demise, you'll be disappointed."

"You'll outlive us all." Gavin bent to kiss her cheek. "I'm happy to see you, at any rate."

"Hmpf."

"Come, now! This is no way to greet your favorite nephew. I've come all the way from Barbados, risking life and limb to visit you." She hadn't invited him to sit, but he disposed his long limbs in the wing chair opposite her and removed his hat, placing it on a handy whatnot. Aunt Agnes watched him with a gleam in her eye that might have been amusement or might have been malice.

"You are my favorite nephew, in point of fact," she remarked, pulling her lap robe higher. "But then, you are my only nephew."

"Had you a dozen nephews, I'd still be your favorite."

She chuckled. "You always were a rascal. I like that in a boy."

"I am no longer a boy."

"When you reach my age—if you ever do— you'll realize that all men are boys. Never mind that. I heard you tell Murdock you're Sir Gavin now."

He inclined his head in a bow of acknowledgement. "I am," he said quietly. "My father passed in August."

"Why was I not told?" she asked sharply.

"I am telling you now. In person."

Aunt Agnes snatched up a handkerchief and began to cough violently. Gavin waited politely. When she recovered, her eyes were watering. He assumed it was the cough, not grief, that had summoned tears. No one had liked his father much.

"I am sorry for your loss," she wheezed.

"Thank you."

"What will you do now? I suppose you inherited his plantation, or whatever you call it." She waved her handkerchief vaguely. "Sugar, isn't it?"

"It was. Acres and acres and acres of sugar. But I've sold them." He smiled blandly. "The West Indies did not agree with me."

Aunt Agnes' eyebrows climbed. "Sold already! You must have acted quickly."

"My father's death was not unexpected. I had time to put his affairs in order. And mine."

Aunt Agnes leaned back against the settee. Her hooded eyes gleamed and her lips twisted wryly. "I daresay you want Ashwood Hall."

"Indeed I do."

"Be careful what you wish for. Your father couldn't afford Ashwood without my money."

Gavin felt his jaw clench. *Her* money. He devoutly hoped his Uncle Jasper was suffering somewhere in the afterlife for that. "I can, however."

"Ha." A look of deep satisfaction settled across her aquiline features. "So Monty made his fortune after all."

"Just as he intended."

"Why did he not come back?"

26

"My father liked Barbados. And, as you say, he was successful. A man of his stamp does not easily walk away from success, even to take up life as an English gentleman."

Aunt Agnes gave a short bark of laughter. "That's Monty for you. I daresay he was mightily at home in the jungle."

He opened his mouth to correct her, but closed it again. There was little point in describing the island to Aunt Agnes, whose view of the world would not alter in any case. "As you say, ma'am. But do you mean to leave Ashwood vacant forever? Uncle Jasper would not have approved such a plan."

A shadow passed across her face. "Do not speak to me of Jasper's wishes, you impertinent puppy. You know nothing about them."

"I beg your pardon." He inclined his head, although his eyes never left her face. "But I am right. Ashwood should not stand empty."

Her fingers plucked restlessly at her shawl. "I never intended to leave it empty. But after Jasper passed, I couldn't bear the place. Every room I entered held a hundred memories." She frowned. "I came to Bath for diversion. I did not realize..." Another spasm of coughing seized her and she pressed the handkerchief to her face, frowning over it as if irritated she had said so much. It was unlike Aunt Agnes to admit to tender sentiments. She must be feeling poorly indeed.

Gavin waited respectfully for her to recover her breath. "A house should be lived in, and an estate cannot be run properly from a distance. Hensley is a fine fellow, but you know as well as I do that a dozen decisions must be made every day. They should be made by a DuFrayne and executed by Hensley, not made by Hensley, executed by Hensley, and sent to you in a letter after the fact."

Aunt Agnes pointed to the side table. "Pass me that green vial," she barked. "You seem determined to take advantage of me in my weakened state. I must fortify myself."

He laughed and handed it to her. "Very well, Aunt. But I am proposing nothing out of the ordinary. The heir returns and takes up the reins of his inheritance. It happens every day."

"Not in this family." She poured a dollop of clear liquid from the vial into an empty teacup and sipped it, grimacing. "There's income from the estate, of course, but not enough to live there in the style Ashwood demands. I won't have you moving in and pinching pennies, running the place down."

Gavin smiled, but it was not a pleasant smile. "Allow me to remind you, ma'am, that if I choose to move in, you cannot stop me. The house and land are mine now."

"But not the fortune," she snapped. "You'll not see a farthing of it while I live, and I mean to live for a good while yet." Her eyes gleamed at him over the rim of the teacup. "In point of fact, Gavin, you may not get it when I'm gone. Best you know that now, if you didn't before. The money is mine, to do with as I please. And to leave wherever I choose."

His expression must have given him away. Aunt Agnes gave a grim cackle. "You didn't know that, eh? Assumed Jasper gave me only a life interest? Well, you're wrong. It's mine, free and clear. So if you want to live at Ashwood, I hope your sugar cane brought you a pretty penny."

"Thank you," said Gavin icily. "How I long to tell you it's none of your business."

She laughed herself into another coughing fit. He lifted one of the other cordials on the table between them and looked at her inquiringly, but she waved it away, still coughing. "Useless stuff," she wheezed. "More like to poison than cure me."

"In that case, my dear aunt, allow me to add some to your cup."

She chuckled hoarsely. "I thought I was your favorite aunt."

"You were, until you began to quiz me about money in this vulgar way."

"Practical." She struggled to breathe evenly. "Must be practical. Drat this cough." She set her teacup, now empty again, back on the side table. "Tell me, Gavin. May as well."

Gavin sighed. "Yes. I shall have to inform Hensley of where I stand, and he'll tell you whether I like it or not. Very well, madam. I sold the plantation at a tidy profit, and in combination with the rest of my inheritance I have a little over eighty thousand pounds, safely invested in the three-percents."

Lady DuFrayne's eyes narrowed. "Twenty-four hundred a year, then. Most would call that a comfortable income. But Ashwood is no common property."

He laughed aloud. "Nor is it Buckingham Palace! My notion of comfort may be more modest than yours, Aunt. You are a creature of the last century."

Her lips twitched. "In my day, we knew what was due to our station. You're a generation of parsons, Gavin."

He grinned at her. "If you're worried that my austerity will cause Ashwood to suffer, you may rest easy. If I learned nothing else in Barbados, I learned how to manage vast tracts of land. Of course, if you prefer, I will be happy to direct Hensley to continue sending the bills to you."

"Ha! Unseemly." Lady DuFrayne stuffed a cushion behind her back, coughing. "So will you be haring off to Ashwood now, or do you plan to winter in Bath?"

Gavin bowed. "I was hoping to trespass upon your hospitality, Aunt. I have only brought one manservant, and your house appears large enough to accommodate us."

"I daresay! But for how long?"

"Until you toss me out into the snow."

She chuckled. "A week, then. Two, if it doesn't snow. Three, if you make yourself useful."

"Useful! Will you set me to shoveling coal, or to polishing the teaspoons?"

"I wouldn't trust you with my silver," she said tartly. "But I do have a niece who wants dancing lessons. You can teach her, and save me the trouble of hiring a dancing master."

Startled, Gavin stared at her. "Felicity can't *dance?*"

"Felicity? Of course Felicity dances," the old lady snapped. "It's her wretched sister who needs lessons. I've promised to bring the chit out, and she's raw as an onion. You'll remember her. Lulu."

Gavin cast his mind back and, with difficulty, recalled a plump little girl with boundless energy. "Lulu. Good lord."

"My sentiments precisely. But a promise is a promise."

Gavin's lips tightened as anger began to gnaw at him. Aunt Agnes was sponsoring another Pennington girl. As if her lavish indulgence of Felicity's pretensions were not galling enough, the wretched woman was about to spend thousands more, no doubt, on Lulu. Lulu, of all people! He could not imagine the unattractive tomboy he remembered growing into a girl who could take the *ton* by storm. And anything less would be a shocking waste of money.

DuFrayne money.

30

*His* money, by rights.

He would definitely winter in Bath.

Gavin frowned, unseeing, out the window of Lady DuFrayne's second-best bedchamber. He had made a grave error. Not an irretrievable one, he hoped, but he must tread carefully.

He had not expected Aunt Agnes to relinquish the family fortune to him, of course. She was neither sentimental nor weak, and she relished her new power to infuriate her husband's relatives. Uncle Jasper's sisters had done their level best to snub and undermine her during her marriage, so he did not blame her for cutting them off with a shilling. But he had hoped—foolishly—that her affection for him might override her desire to punish the DuFraynes, at least enough to loosen her purse-strings for a worthy cause.

And then, somehow, he had failed to confide the worthy cause to her.

Less than a week in England, and already its prejudices and provincialism had forced him to rethink his position. Less than half an hour in the presence of his redoubtable aunt, and it was starkly clear that the tenor of her mind was...inelastic. A wry, humorless smile twisted his lips. He could not imagine presenting his case to her. She could no more picture the plight of the people he had left behind than she could empathize with Hottentots. It was too alien, too distant from her own experience of the world. Too...un-English.

A soft knock heralded the entrance of one of those persons of whom he'd been thinking—the only one, thus far, he'd succeeded in rescuing. If rescue it could be called.

David's arms were full of neatly-stacked clothing. He crossed to the wardrobe and began putting Gavin's things away.

"How are you getting on?" asked Gavin. "Did they feed you in the kitchen?"

"Yes, sir." David's expressive, lively face was unusually somber. "But they cannot understand a word I say." It came out *dey canna unnastan a wudda see.* Gavin understood him perfectly and sighed.

"I shall tell them to pretend you are Scottish," he said. "Can you understand them?"

A grin flitted across David's face. "Not so much," he admitted. "But better than they understand me. Don't worry about it, sir. I'll get by. I am a man of consequence in this house, you know."

"Are you?"

"Oh, yes." He shut the wardrobe doors and chuckled. "They call me Mister David."

Gavin chuckled. "I ought to have prepared you. As my personal manservant, your status is higher downstairs than anyone other than Murdock and—what's her ladyship's maid's name? Williams?"

"Am I to call her Williams?"

"By no means. Call her Mrs. Williams, and Murdock Mr. Murdock. The housekeeper and the cook, also, you should call Mister or Missus. The others you may address by their Christian names, I believe." He rubbed his chin. "I may be on shaky ground here. But I think that's right. I'll ask Murdock to help you with the niceties—you being a foreigner and all."

David nodded. "Thank you, sir." He hesitated, then looked quizzically at Gavin. "So what is my name now? Am I David David here?"

Gavin almost winced. "That is entirely my

fault. I told Murdock your name was David, and everyone assumed it was your surname. You were not allowed to have one in Barbados, but here you will need one, my friend. What is your family name? This is a question I ought to have asked you long ago."

David's expression shuttered. He picked up a handkerchief, already folded, and began refolding it with more than usual care, staring down at the crisp, white folds. "When your name be taken from you, it is not so easy to get back," he said softly. "I do not know my family name. My people were Ashanti. But that is not our name, you know. It is a tribe."

Gavin nodded. "I have heard of it. What of your wife? Is she Ashanti too?"

"She is Eboe." He grinned. "But if I take it as my name, my wife will be Ashanti. She will be Sally Ashanti."

"So you wish to take David Ashanti as your name?"

"I thought of other names, you know, more like the English sound. I could be Mr. Freeman. I could be Mr. Winter, since I first come here in winter. But why? I am no Englishman."

"It is well thought of." Gavin strolled to the table by the window, where a silver tray bore glasses and a stoppered bottle. He poured two tots and handed one to his manservant with an air of great formality, then toasted him. "To David Ashanti," he intoned. "Long may he live and greatly may he prosper on this side of the sea."

The newly-christened Mr. Ashanti lifted his glass, smiling widely. When they finished, he set his glass back on the tray and softly ran one finger around its crystal rim. "I never thought I'd live to see the day, sir," he said softly. "I thank you."

"Pshaw. You'd have done the same for me."

"I would that. Never doubt it."

"I hope you fit in well, David—though I should call you Ashanti now—and make a friend or two in Bath."

"It be more better when Sally come."

"That may be months from now."

"I understand, sir. I look forward to the day." David gestured to a small door at the side of the room. "They put me in a little room right there, you know. So I can give you a shout if I get scared in the night."

Gavin laughed. "Bath is not a scary place, my friend."

The fleeting grin appeared again. "Not to you."

## Chapter Three

The next day, Gavin headed toward Lady DuFrayne's music room, lured by the muffled sound of laughter and someone thumping loudly on her ladyship's pianoforte. He opened the door in time to see Felicity Pennington dragging a short, towheaded girl across the polished hardwood floor. The girl was simpering affectedly, batting her lashes and cooing while Felicity whooped with laughter.

"No, no, no!" exclaimed Felicity, still laughing. "In rhythm, Lulu!"

Both the music and the laughter halted abruptly when he entered. "Don't mind me," said Gavin modestly. "I came in search of my fan. I dropped it somewhere during the quadrille—"

"Oh, Gavin, how absurd you are," said Felicity, blushing furiously. "I am sorry if we disturbed you."

"Not at all." He bowed to the dark-haired, suspicious-looking girl at the pianoforte. "It's Helena, isn't it? How do you do?"

She shot him a wary glance, mumbled "I'm well, thank you," and dropped her eyes to the keyboard before her. *Shy,* he thought, and pitied her.

Felicity advanced, self-consciously smoothing her hair. "And this is Lulu, of course," she said, indicating the little blonde. Lulu had turned very pink and was biting her lip, but she when Gavin bowed she managed to drop a nervous curtsey.

"Of course," said Gavin. "I remember you well. You were thirteen or fourteen, I think, when last I saw you, and wore your hair in plaits."

"Yes," said Lulu. "You used to sneak up behind me and tug them."

"Did I?" said Gavin, startled.

Felicity patted Lulu's shoulder. "That was when he was a boy and you were a wee thing."

"It apparently made a lasting impression," remarked Gavin. Not on him, however. "I beg your pardon."

"Then I beg yours," said Lulu. "For punching you in the arm whenever you did it."

"That will do," said Felicity quickly. Her color was rising again. "Your fist was too small at the time to do any damage."

"Lucky for me," said Gavin. He rubbed his hands together, looking round the room. It was a beautiful room, but unnecessarily gloomy with the curtains drawn against the cold. He strode to the window embrasure and flung back the heavy folds blocking the light. "Did you ring for a fire? I'd as lief dance in an icehouse."

Felicity raised an eyebrow. "Are you joining us?"

"Joining you? I'm leading you." He bowed with a flourish. "Aunt Agnes said you needed a caper-merchant and asked if I would fill the position. As I am otherwise unemployed, I jumped at the offer."

Felicity's eyes lit with amusement. "In that case, pray ring for a fire! We do not like to spend Aunt Agnes's money on trifles, but a fire will likely be the only wage you receive. And of course you are accustomed to warmer climes. You mustn't risk your health merely to teach Lulu a few steps."

Lulu and Helena were wearing thick pelisses and Felicity was in a cranberry-colored redingote, buttoned to her throat. It was interesting, he thought, that they had preferred to practice dancing in their outerwear rather than trouble Lady DuFrayne's staff. Were they really concerned for her purse? Gavin had to bite his tongue to keep from pointing out that a London Season was considerably more expensive than a bucket of coal. He supposed Felicity would tell him one was necessary and the other was not.

While waiting for the fire to take hold, he kept warm by teaching Lulu the steps of Sir Gilbert Go Softly. Felicity helpfully played the role of second couple, beseeching Lulu to employ her imagination to fill in the long row of invisible dancers standing two-by-two behind her, but Lulu kept breaking into giggles.

"This will not serve," said Felicity at last. "We need more dancers."

"Never mind," said Lulu. "I know a great many country dances already."

"Do you waltz?" Gavin asked.

"Not—not to speak of. No." She was biting her lip again.

"Excellent. It will be easier to teach you a two-person dance," said Gavin. "Helena, do you have music? Anything in three-quarter time will do." While Helena dug through her music stack, he took Lulu firmly, but lightly, in his arms. It was impossible to find her waist beneath the pelisse, but he did his best. "No, place your hand in mine. Thus."

The poor girl had turned red as a beet and was staring fixedly at his topmost coat button.

"Relax, Lulu," he said cheerfully. "You are among family, are you not?" He attempted to steer her through the simple pattern of steps, but her obvious discomfort made her stiff and clumsy. Helena added music, but it did not help; Lulu's feet could not seem to follow where he led. The fire was now glowing in the grate and he suggested she remove her pelisse—which she did, albeit reluctantly. He could then find her waist easily and more clearly see what she was doing wrong, but if anything her nervousness increased, and every suggestion he made seemed to increase her distress.

"I am hopeless," she cried at last.

"Nonsense," he said firmly. "Merely a trifle stiff. It will go easier if you—"

"It will go easier if I watch you first." She pulled out of his grasp and put her hands behind her back, refusing to take another step with him. "Please, Sir Gavin. Could you do it once with Felicity—very slowly?"

Felicity paused in the act of unbuttoning her redingote. Was that reluctance he spied in her eyes? Puzzled, Gavin held out his hand to her. "Come, Cousin," he said. "Your sisterly duty calls."

Her smile was perfunctory. "Very well." She laid her coat on a nearby chair, where she had already deposited her gloves, took a deep breath, and joined him. Her ungloved hand was warm and surprisingly soft. Gavin's eyes met hers for the barest of moments; she dropped her eyes immediately. Her slender fingers trembled slightly in his. Was she shy of him for some reason? It was most unlike the Felicity Pennington he had known.

Her odd reaction to his touch, subtle as it was, surprised Gavin into looking at her with fresh eyes. He had always thought of her as a skinny brunette with no claim to beauty. But her dark hair was smooth and rich, and arranged becomingly. Her creamy complexion glowed with good health. Her lashes were long and her mouth was soft. As for the nose, about which he used to tease her unmercifully—well, it was still there. But he was willing to concede that it gave her face character. Her body was slim and supple but she was not the bony, angular girl she had been when he last saw her, and her simple morning dress had that indefinable something that drew the eye. She had taste, he realized. She had flair. She had *ton.*

It was possible, he suddenly recognized, that she had not been bony and angular five years ago either. He may have never looked properly at her, recalling her only as the coltish child he'd teased and laughed with at Ashwood. Such good friends they had been. Nostalgia tugged at him, remembering the two of them exploring the woods, running races on the lawn, playing absurd games of their own invention, and talking long into the evening. What had they talked about, he wondered. It had never seemed to matter. Felicity made everything interesting.

What a pity that the simple friendships of youth faded away, replaced with more complicated relationships. Relationships that were not more satisfying than his with Felicity had been—merely different.

The dark lashes resting against her cheek swept up. One slim brow arched. Her grey eyes were meeting his again, with the old laughter lurking in their depths. "Can't recall the steps?" she said. "Or have you merely fallen asleep?"

Blast. He'd been standing like a stick, lost in reverie.

"Neither," he said promptly. "I am trying to decide which of the nine figures is simplest to demonstrate."

"You are out of date," she informed him kindly. "There are sixteen figures."

"There will be twenty by the time we finish," he promised. "You and I will invent a few, and take the *ton* by storm." He lifted both her hands and hooked his pinkies with hers. "This, for example, is destined to be all the rage by April." He nodded at Helena for music and began circling the floor face-to-face with Felicity, holding their hands solemnly aloft, pinkies linked, while Lulu giggled.

"This hold is terrible. I cannot tell which way to go," Felicity complained.

"Nonsense. You are following admirably. But by all means, let us try another figure." He abruptly dropped her hands and slid one arm around her waist. She stumbled, startled, as he pulled her to him, and caught at his shoulders for balance.

Felicity's face was suddenly very close to his. Their eyes met and held. Her lips were parted, and he struggled not to stare at her mouth. The music continued, but he realized dimly that they had stopped dancing. He was intensely aware of the warmth of her body, of the slim waist beneath his hand and the clean fragrance of soap and starch and, well, Felicity.

He had not intended to pull her quite so close. And, having done it, he certainly had not expected this odd rush of sensual awareness that made him reluctant to let go. The moment was not long, but it seemed long. She pushed gently on his shoulders and stepped back with a breathless little laugh.

"Mark it, Lulu—when a gentleman pulls you excessively close, it becomes obvious which way he intends to lead you."

"Into temptation." Gavin grinned. "It's all

part of the dance." He adjusted their position to a more chaste version of the hold and whirled Felicity round and round, steering her lightly by one hand at her waist and the other clasping hers. "It can be danced this way, too," he called to Lulu, shifting again to place both hands at Felicity's waist. She clung to his upper arms for a few moments, then pressed her palms against his collarbone, compelling him to keep a respectable distance. He laughed at her. "Do you shove gentlemen away by brute force? No wonder you are still single."

"How rude of you to mention that," she said, seeming resigned. "I'd forgotten how uncivil you are."

He twirled her with a flourish, then grabbed her by the elbows. She laid her forearms along his and held his elbows too, wrinkling her nose. "Gavin, nobody waltzes this way anymore." But still they circled, face-to-face, not missing a beat. She really did follow him admirably.

"This figure is popular in Kingston," he said untruthfully, placing one hand over his eyes.

"What am I to do?"

"Hold me by the lapels." And with one hand over his eyes and the other at her waist, he attempted to steer Felicity as she clung to his lapels, laughing.

"Mind the furniture! You ought to let me lead."

"Never," he said firmly. "Ouch." He had crashed them into a small table at the side of the room.

"How charming Kingston society must be," Felicity mused. "I shall visit one day and watch them waltz."

"You should," said Gavin, rubbing his knee. "It's a spectacle best viewed from a distance, actually."

"I see that."

The lesson immediately devolved into a series of ridiculous new ways to dance the waltz, as Gavin and Felicity each tried to top the other in proposing silly postures and ever-more-difficult ways to hold one's partner. Lulu laughed so hard she ended up in a heap on the floor, and even Helena giggled as Gavin and Felicity solemnly circled the room back-to-back, then at arm's length, then with Felicity clinging to the tail of Gavin's coat.

"You see, Lulu?" Gavin said at last. "It's all in the footwork."

"Which you, as the lady, need not mind overmuch," added Felicity. "The man will lead and you merely follow. If you manage to do so without stepping on his toes or crashing into the furniture, voilà! You have danced the waltz."

The absurdity was, Lulu actually performed much better after watching her sister mock the waltz with him. She must have been tense after all, and the laughter eased her nerves. She never mastered the steps, but learned to smile and keep her head up—at Felicity's suggestion—which gave the illusion that she was perfectly competent, whatever her feet were doing. Felicity assured her that many a lady had no more notion than she how the waltz should properly be danced.

"Do you think that's true?" Gavin murmured to Felicity, as they trooped downstairs to take luncheon with Aunt Agnes.

"No," she replied softly. "But I saw no point in pressing her further. Lulu has a great deal of energy, but no..." she paused. "Finesse," she concluded with a sigh.

Gavin nodded. He'd reached much the same conclusion. If Aunt Agnes managed to marry this girl off, it would be a miracle.

When they reached the dining room, where Murdock had set out a cold collation, Lady DuFrayne's sharp eyes were on them at once. "Sit down, all of you. Lulu on my right, please. How was your lesson?"

Lulu did as she was bade, but looked ready to sink beneath the table. "It—it was fine, Aunt Agnes," she stammered. "Very, um, very..."

"Sit up straight," commanded Aunt Agnes. "And don't mumble. Did Gavin help you or not?"

"He did," said Gavin firmly.

"He did," Lulu echoed.

Beside him, Felicity was smiling into her serviette. Gavin raised an eyebrow at her. "Did I not?"

She returned the serviette to her lap. "I assure you, Aunt Agnes, that the lesson was worth every penny you paid for it."

"Hmpf," said the old lady, but her eyes were twinkling. "I paid not a farthing, as well you know. Sounded like a herd of elephants trampling my music room. Who played? Helena?"

Helena swallowed. "Yes, ma'am."

"You play well," said Aunt Agnes. "One day I shall give you some music worth playing. Murdock! Remind me to purchase sheet music for my niece."

"Yes, madam."

Gavin helped himself to a liberal serving of shaved ham and observed, with sympathy, Lulu enduring Aunt Agnes's scrutiny. The sharp-tongued old woman soon had her shy niece reduced to stammering idiocy and, beside him, Felicity's expression was darkening to a thunderous aspect. He intervened before the storm could break.

"I wonder, Aunt, if you should quiz the tutor rather than the pupil."

As he had intended her to do, Lady

DuFrayne diverted her attention from Lulu and pinned her basilisk glare on Gavin. "It is the pupil whose debut I am franking."

"True. But for a first lesson, I thought your niece did well. You need not fear that she will embarrass you."

Her ladyship gave an inelegant snort and speared a grape with her fork. "I fear nothing, Sir Cheek. I merely feel a duty to spare the Polite World the necessity of welcoming a lummox, out of regard for me."

Up came Felicity's head. "Lulu is not—"

"I did not say she was," snapped Aunt Agnes. "I am aware, Felicity, of your opinion on this subject. And I shall not go back on my word at any rate."

Felicity wisely bit back whatever it was she intended to say and returned her attention to the bread and lettuce on her plate. Lulu, however, astonished the company by speaking up—despite having turned a remarkable shade of pink. "I may be a lummox, Aunt Agnes," she said, with great dignity, "but I shall do my best. I am very sensible of the honor you are bestowing on me, and yes, I am grateful too. I will not repay your kindness by disgracing you in the eyes of your friends."

Surprise held Gavin and Felicity motionless, with forks suspended mid-air, but Lady DuFrayne gave Lulu a grim nod of approval. "Well said, child," she said, in a milder tone. "I am aware, thanks to your sister, that I can be rather...quelling." She directed a sharp glance at Felicity, and humor once again gleamed in her eyes. "I daresay you do not appear at your best when I snap at you. I shall endeavor to remember it."

Lulu seemed to breathe again. "Thank you, ma'am," she said meekly.

The old lady gave a bark of laughter. "You

don't deny it, then."

"No, ma'am."

"Hm! Well, keep your courage up if you can. Bear in mind that none of the *ton* will bite you."

"At least not literally," said Felicity, her equanimity apparently restored. "I am confident that after your adventure you shall return to Bath unscathed."

*And unwed,* thought Gavin, although he said nothing. And tried, unsuccessfully, to put out of his mind the thought of all the money Aunt Agnes was about to pour blithely down the drain.

## Chapter Four

*Miss Lucille Pennington.* Lulu ran her fingertip reverently over the delicate lettering. How lovely her name looked, printed perfectly in the center of that white rectangle. Surely the owner of such an elegant calling card would have an innate grace, a dignity that matched the smooth, sloping script. First impressions are everything, she told herself. With her newly-printed cards, she would make an impression that was ... well ... impressive.

Tonight, she promised herself, would be a night of transformation. She would no longer be Lulu, the butt of every family joke. She would bid farewell to clumsy, silly, luckless Lulu, and become Miss Lucille Pennington, lady of refinement, admired by all. The calling card would change her luck. She would carry it as a talisman. *Miss Lucille Pennington.*

Of course, she didn't need a talisman if she kept her wits about her. Other young ladies navigated the social scene with ease, and so could she. It was simply a matter of practice.

With these optimistic thoughts, she tucked the beautiful little card back into her reticule. It was an evening reticule, not much bigger than the calling card, so it took some time for her gloved fingers to work the silken strings loose and shove the card in. She had to be careful to neither tangle the strings nor bend the card—

"What are you doing?" said Felicity's voice, very suddenly and quite close behind her. Lulu jumped, squeaked, and clutched the card. "Isn't that one of your calling cards?"

Lulu stared glumly down at the formerly-pristine scrap of paperboard. Now a deep crease ran right through the center of her name. "It was."

Felicity gave an indulgent chuckle. "Goose. The calling cards are for morning visits."

"I realize that," said Lulu, with dignity. "I was carrying it for luck." The crease looked as if someone had struck a line through her name. It didn't seem a particularly good omen. She felt her optimism wavering.

"Lulu, darling, you won't need luck tonight," said her sister confidently. "Nothing will go amiss."

She devoutly hoped that Felicity was right. She was rather of the opinion that she did need luck. Heaps and heaps of luck. She didn't really believe in signs and omens—much. She just wanted all the help she could get. A calling card was less bulky than a rabbit's foot. On the other hand, a rabbit's foot would have been sturdier. Oh, well.

She stuffed the card into her reticule. "I shall keep it with me anyway," she remarked. "In case I forget my name."

Felicity laughed, then cast a quick glance about. The sisters were alone. Voices and music could be heard coming from the adjoining rooms, but there was no one else in Aunt Agnes's echoing marble foyer. "Let me look at you again."

Lulu obediently stood back and let her sister run her eyes over her. "Perfect," declared Felicity at last. Her shoulders visibly relaxed. "Not a hair out of place. Not a smidgen of dirt. Not a speck of dust. Not a rip, not a crease." The note of congratulation in her voice signaled that she had not, actually, expected this much from Lulu. "You don't need luck, my dear—you merely need to pay attention." A look of anxiety crossed her features. "Whatever happens tonight, for heaven's sake, don't let anything distract you. Don't get interested in anything."

"I won't," Lulu promised fervently. "I shall be the soul of elegance, unmovable and languid and bored by everything, no matter how interesting it is. I shall behave just as if I were made of wax. You won't recognize me."

"Excellent." Apparently unaware of the insult lurking in her brief word of approval, Felicity gave Lulu's shoulder a reassuring pat. "Here we go, then."

She started toward Aunt Agnes's drawing room, but Lulu hung back. Now that the moment had actually arrived, panic fluttered along her nerves. She swallowed hard, trying to will her nervousness away. If only this didn't matter so much! She wished, now, that she had not remembered that saying about first impressions. She had never made a decent first impression in her life. It seemed unlikely she would suddenly succeed where she had so often failed.

"Would—would you go in before me?" she begged. "I think I would like to collect my thoughts. Just for a moment or two."

Surprise flickered in Felicity's eyes, then understanding. "Of course," she said gently. "But don't be nervous, Lulu. You'll do splendidly. You look very pretty."

Lulu gave her a wavering smile. She felt a pang of envy as Felicity swept gracefully out of the room. She wished she had Felicity's poise. She wished she had a tenth of Felicity's poise.

She took a deep breath then exhaled slowly, straightening her spine. The Season won't begin until spring, she reminded herself. By then, she would have poise aplenty. Her Bath debut was nothing but a rehearsal. "Miss Lucille Pennington," she whispered, to give herself courage.

Alone in the foyer, she minced daintily across the marble floor, practicing. She pictured the amazement, the approval, the dawning respect of everyone who knew her, as the New Lulu—no, Lucille—blossomed before their eyes. Hope and confidence rose in her once more.

She stretched out her hand like a cardinal expecting to have his ring kissed. "Miss Lucille Pennington," she said haughtily. "Of the Bath Penningtons, you know." And then she clapped her hand over her mouth to stifle the laugh that bubbled up.

It *was* ridiculous, to picture herself among the *haut ton*. But since she must do it, it helped to know that she could look as elegant as she did tonight. Her blonde curls had been cropped and tamed, her complexion glowed from a week's nightly application of Denmark Lotion, and her gown was made of silk. Silk! She had never before been trusted with anything so expensive. Her reticule, beaded to match the trim on her dress— and so fashionably tiny that it served no useful purpose whatsoever—dangled from one wrist. Her slippers matched her gloves. Why, she looked like a princess.

Now all she had to do was behave like one.

She faced the drawing room, took one last, deep breath and glided forward, her gait self-consciously smooth. But then she noticed the flowers.

The sight brought her up short as an idea flashed in her brain. A wonderful, luck-enhancing idea. She stared at the flowers, an eager smile breaking across her features.

An enormous vase—an urn, actually—stood high in a niche in the foyer wall, packed with the most beautiful flower arrangement Lulu had ever seen. Such flowers did not bloom in winter, so of course they were artificial. But there they were, and they were gorgeous, and *they matched Lulu's gown.*

Delight shot through her. This more than made up for the mashed calling card. The flowers were better than a talisman; since she had had nothing to do with placing them there, they must be an *omen!* This was too, too perfect for coincidence. Tonight would be her lucky night after all.

Feeling absurdly cheered, Lulu approached the niche. Aunt Agnes would not mind, she knew, if she borrowed a sprig. If she took a tiny one, from the back of the arrangement, it would not be missed. She felt quite sure it would bring her luck. And even if it didn't bring her luck, it would look well in her hair.

There were several spindle-legged chairs set at intervals along the wall. She dragged the nearest one below the niche, gathered up her skirts, and stood on it. It hardly wobbled at all, and brought her face level with the base of the urn. Encouraged, she went up on tiptoe to reach the very back, determined that her efforts not spoil the front of the arrangement. She extended her arm carefully past all the perfectly-set flowers and closed her gloved fingers, very gently, around a pretty little spray in the rear of the group. Then she tugged.

The flowers were real.

The brass urn was full of water.

Lulu realized both these things in the same instant that she realized the flowers, and the water, had made the urn top-heavy. Her harmless little tug overset the urn's precarious balance. Lulu's balance was precarious as well, since she had stretched up on tiptoe. She tried frantically to catch the urn with her outstretched arm, but only succeeded in aiming it squarely at herself as it fell. An avalanche of flowers descended, borne on a river of cold water. Lulu toppled backwards off the chair and landed on the marble floor, covered with flowers and drenched to the skin, with the empty urn uselessly clutched to her chest.

Time seemed to stop in its tracks. In that instant—that frightful, heart-stopping, miserable instant—Lulu had time to think these bitter words: *of course.* The part of her that was forever braced for disaster, the part of her that knew she was unlucky and that her luck would never, ever, change, whispered those mocking words to her. *Of course.* She should have known this would happen. This, or something like it. She should have known.

She allowed herself one horrified gasp. Then she sat up, set the urn on the floor, and began gathering the scattered flowers as quickly as she could. This was the one useful trait a lifetime of disaster had eventually bestowed on her: the ability to act quickly in a crisis.

She had caught the urn in her arms— upended, unfortunately, so the contents had emptied onto her—but it might have been worse. At least she had cushioned it with her body so it did not crash onto the floor. Had it done so, the racket might have brought the household running to the scene, completing her humiliation. As it was, if she could only put the flowers back the way they were—

Her frantic, chilled fingers, hampered by wet gloves, were dropping the flowers as fast as she could pick them up. *Don't panic,* she told herself sternly, trying to slow down her racing, shaking hands. Most of the flowers had survived with no visible damage. All she need do was return them to the vase and place the vase back in the niche.

Then (she told herself bitterly) she could crawl off to some dark hole, wait for the pneumonia she would inevitably catch to set in, and die in peace.

The flowers did not look quite the same when she had finished cramming them into the urn, but at least she finally managed to get them all in. Only then did she glance behind her ... and see the pool of water spreading slowly across Aunt Agnes's polished floor.

At home, Lulu knew where every mop and broom was kept, but she had no notion where to find such items in Lady DuFrayne's magnificent abode. Well, she must try. She would expire with embarrassment if she had to tell one of Aunt Agnes's starchy footmen to fetch a mop and clean up her mess.

She had taken only a step or two when a blur of movement caught the edge of her vision. There was no time to cry out a warning; someone was rounding the corner. Lulu whirled, instinctively trying to catch the person before they slipped in the water. Too late! Her body collided, hard, with that of a total stranger. Together, they executed a kind of pirouette. Then, down they both went.

She landed face-down on the stranger's chest, clutching his coat sleeves. His chest was wide and solid, and she could feel his biceps bunching beneath her hands as he grabbed at her to steady her. She lifted her head and a pair of startled eyes—hazel, she noted distractedly, and quite nice—met hers. She was lying on the chest of a very attractive man. Rather a young man. And a gentleman, too.

*Oh, no.*

This was worse than anything. If only she had fallen on a female. Or a servant. Or an old family friend. Anyone, *anyone*, other than a handsome stranger.

Mortified, she struggled to free herself. He held her in a grip of iron. "Sorry," she panted, agonized. "I'm so sorry."

"Are you all right?"

"Y-yes. Oh!" It was an exclamation of remorse; he had winced as her knee dug into his thigh. "Sorry."

"Not at all." His voice sounded a bit strained. "My fault entirely." He did not let her go. He seemed to be under the impression that Lulu needed his assistance to rise. He held her firmly, cradling her against his chest as he tried to roll sideways. Lulu, knowing he would be rolling into the gigantic puddle, resisted. They struggled mutely for a few seconds. Then he noticed the water. He stopped trying to roll her sideways, but held her even more tightly. "'Ware the floor," he warned. "It's wet."

Lulu felt her cheeks begin to burn. "Yes, it is. I'm frightfully sorry." She made one more attempt to rise.

"Elbow," he gasped.

"Oh, dear." She collapsed back onto his chest. "Sorry."

An extraordinary expression crossed his features. "It's seeping through my coat."

"Oh, I am *so* sorry—" She squirmed desperately, trying to change places with him.

"What the—what are you trying to do?"

"Move you away from the water."

"My dear girl, stop that at once. You'll end up in the puddle."

"I am already wet. Pray you, lie still!" She tried again, more forcefully. Taken by surprise, the stranger failed to prevent her this time. But since he still did not let her go, they performed a barrel roll together. Lulu ended up beneath him.

The stranger, with a muttered exclamation of outraged chivalry, rolled underneath her again, returning himself to the watery floor and placing Lulu back on top.

She kept her temper, but barely. The man was stubborn to a fault. "Sir," she said patiently, as if explaining the situation to an idiot, "you are mopping the floor with your coat."

"You seem determined to mop it with your gown."

"I had *rather* mop it with my gown."

"That's absurd."

"No, it isn't. My gown is already wet."

"Then you won't be able to mop with it, will you? Hold still."

"Sir!" She struggled futilely against his grip. "Allow me to make what amends I can."

"I see no reason why you should make amends at all." To Lulu's amazement, a spark of laughter seemed to have entered the gentleman's eyes. He must be daft. "Our predicament is mutual."

"Yes, but the predicament is not your fault!"

"Never mind. I am a gentleman and you are a lady. It falls to me, therefore, to extricate us."

"Sir, you are not extricating us. You are making a bad situation worse! Release my arms, if you please."

"If I do, you will attempt once more to mop the floor with your gown."

"I will attempt to *rise.*"

"That is evidently the same thing." He shook his head regretfully. "I'm afraid I can't allow it."

She glared at him. "You are simply being difficult."

"Am I?" A delighted smile crinkled the edges of his hazel eyes. "You may be correct. How extraordinary. I am normally not a difficult sort of person. In fact—"

"Oh, for pity's sake!" The gentleman seemed inclined to *converse* with her, while lying beneath her on the floor! She dug her elbows into his ribcage, ignoring his muffled yelp, and struggled free of his grip. She landed in the puddle, naturally, but at least she was sitting.

He sat up too, looking around them for the first time. "What a shambles."

"So I have told you." Three broken-stemmed lilies lay crushed between them. One had streaked the gentleman's black pantaloons with yellow pollen. Tears stung Lulu's eyes. She bit her tongue to keep from adding to her shame by weeping like a child. She picked up the lilies and tried to shake the water from their ruined petals.

"My dear girl—ah, that is, my dear young lady—what are you doing?"

"Putting them back, of course." She brushed futilely at her ruined silk skirt, trying to get the worst of the water off it.

With an exclamation, the gentleman sprang up—rather nimbly, for a man of his square build—and pulled her to her feet. "No, really, I say! We must summon assistance. You cannot put this to rights. And I shan't tease you anymore," he said, smiling. "Unhandsome of me, wasn't it?"

Unhandsome. That wasn't quite the word Lulu had in mind. In fact, his smile made him so much the opposite of unhandsome, she could not think of a single word to say in reply. He had the nicest smile she had ever seen. Unable to make an intelligent response, she simply gulped and nodded.

While she collected her wits, the gentleman's gaze studied the urn. Stuffed with slightly mangled flowers, it stood at the edge of what remained of the puddle—now mostly absorbed by Lulu's and the gentleman's clothing. Beside the puddle lay a spindle-legged chair. Above the urn yawned an empty niche. It was fairly obvious what had happened, especially since Lulu's attempt at arranging the flowers had largely failed. The flowers looked, as indeed they were, jammed into the urn with more haste than taste. Lulu watched, her heart sinking, as the gentleman put two and two together.

"You see, it is all my fault," she said in a contrite rush. "I accidentally pulled the flowers down. And spilled the water, of course, in the process. I'm so sorry. I suppose it is absurd to keep telling you how sorry I am, but I—I cannot seem to help it. It is all so ... embarrassing." Her voice sank into a shamed whisper at the end.

The gentleman straightened his coat. He tugged at his cravat. He cleared his throat. He seemed to be struggling with himself—whether to keep his temper or his gravity, she hardly knew. Would he laugh at her? Would he berate her? Either reaction would be horrid, but she could scarcely blame him. His coat, Lulu now saw, was sopping wet all down the back. Lulu hastily averted her gaze, burning with mortification.

"Well," said the gentleman thoughtfully. He still did not look at her. "I was ready to pretend, if you liked, that I believed a careless servant was responsible for the accident. But now that you have honored me with your candor, I suppose I can't go that route." He then favored her with another smile that made her heart turn over.

"Oh," said Lulu faintly. She knew she was blushing. "No. I suppose not. How—how shortsighted of me."

He opened his mouth to reply, but whatever he had been about to say, he did not say. The words seemed to visibly evaporate, forgotten even as he was forming them. His jaw went slack. He stared. Lulu saw his eyes dilate as he gazed at her, as if he had swallowed an enormous dose of laudanum that had just now taken hold. What on earth—?

Bewildered, she realized he was no longer looking into her face. She glanced down at herself, following where his eyes had led. And she felt her own mouth open into a horrified 0 as she beheld, for the first time, the spectacular effect of cold water poured over thin silk.

Lulu's bodice had been rendered transparent.

This was, without a doubt, the worst moment of her life.

His beautifully-tailored evening coat, worn for the first time tonight, was soaked down the back from shoulder to hip. His dignity was in tatters. His evening was probably ruined. And none of it mattered a damn.

He stared. He couldn't help it. The lady was a plump little thing, but she was plump in the right places. It was worth a good soaking, to catch a glimpse of such magnificence.

A glimpse was all he received before the lady crossed her arms protectively over her chest, but that was enough for the tantalizing image to burn itself into his brain. He was well aware that the memory would torment him later.

And that would be worth it, too.

Even though it was none of his business—now that he had settled on Almeria—it cheered a man to discover that feminine perfection existed. And in Bath, of all places.

"My friends assured me Bath would be dull," he mused aloud. "I can't wait to tell them how wrong they were."

The lady flushed to the roots of her hair. The effect was adorable. With her arms still crossed over her chest, she lifted her chin and looked daggers at him. "I am delighted," she said sarcastically, "to have alleviated your boredom."

He felt a stab of contrition. "I think I should lend you my coat. Come and help me out of it." She looked doubtfully at him. He could not repress a grin. "I promise to avert my eyes."

He did, but it was deuced difficult to resist the temptation to peek. He caught himself wondering what Almeria would look like, drenched in water. The fact that he couldn't even imagine Almeria drenched in water was strangely depressing. He banished the thought and returned his attention to the task at hand.

It took their combined strength to unpeel his wet coat. It had been tailored to fit him closely in the first place, and the water had glued it to his body like a second skin. They accomplished it at last, however, and the lady pulled it quickly around herself like a shawl, letting the sleeves hang loose. They dangled nearly to her knees.

She shot a shy, almost frightened, look at him, then quickly turned her face away. "I think—I think the ladies' retiring room is down this passage. I shall put myself in order, sir, and return your coat to you forthwith."

So formal! She was obviously mortified.

"Before you abscond with my coat, I wonder if you would do me the honor of divulging your name? Mine is Stanhope. Oliver Stanhope." He bowed. "At your service."

She dipped in a fraction of a curtsey, still refusing to meet his eyes. "My name is—" She hesitated. He could have sworn she was struggling to remember her own name. How odd. Then, unaccountably, her eyes filled with tears. "I'm *Lulu*," she blurted, as if hating the sound of it. And she fled.

Chapter Five

Lady DuFrayne's drawing room was full of elegantly-dressed persons; the cream of Bath society with a few old family friends to make Lulu feel comfortable. Violins played discreetly in one corner, accompanying the light chatter of genteel conversation. Lady DuFrayne was holding court in a high-backed armchair near the fire. Everyone seemed at ease and among friends, and the party was humming along nicely.

The only missing piece was Lulu. Felicity was trapped in conversation with Mrs. Stanhope, the bishop's wife, and could scarcely cut the woman short to chase down her absent sister. But it was difficult to concentrate on pleasantries while worried about Lulu's apparent stage fright.

From the corner of her eye, she saw Murdock approaching with his most dignified tread, bearing a note on a salver. Her heart sank. In Felicity's experience, messages deemed sufficiently urgent to interrupt a social gathering rarely conveyed good news. She braced herself, certain the note was a distress signal from Lulu— but to her surprise, Murdock bowed to Mrs. Stanhope instead. "For you, Madam," he intoned.

"Gracious," murmured Mrs. Stanhope. "Thank you." She took the folded scrap of paper and, with a murmured apology to Felicity, swiftly read it. Felicity watched as the woman's smile faded to bewilderment. "Dear me."

"Not bad news, I hope?"

"Well, no, not—that is—yes, but nothing serious." She seemed flustered. "I'm afraid my son Oliver will not be joining us tonight after all."

"I'm so sorry," said Felicity. "We had looked forward to meeting him. I hope he was not taken ill?"

Mrs. Stanhope murmured some inaudible reply, her eyes seeking her husband. He started toward them in response to her signal just as a loud burst of feminine laughter, quickly stifled, erupted from a knot of young ladies near the drawing room door.

Felicity misliked the scandalized note in that laughter. She liked even less the sight of four or five girlish heads bent close together, whispering. She looked instinctively toward her aunt and saw that formidable dame glaring at the same gossiping girls that had drawn her own attention. Beside her, the bishop was reading the note his wife had received. His expression conveyed affronted disapproval. Filled with a growing sense of dread, Felicity murmured an excuse and slipped away to join Aunt Agnes by the fire.

"Something's amiss," said Aunt Agnes grimly. "Where's that Lulu?"

"I can't imagine," confessed Felicity. "I'd best go find her. She'll hide from anyone else."

She found her in the first place she looked. One glance at her wet and miserable sister, huddled in the cloakroom with a gentleman's tailcoat draped over her shoulders, and Felicity sent the cloakroom attendant scurrying to fetch Williams, Lady DuFrayne's personal maid. Together they spirited Lulu upstairs to Lady

DuFrayne's dressing room, stripped her down to her chemise, and stood her before the fire to dry. Williams vanished with Lulu's discarded garments and the gentleman's coat, promising to perform whatever miracles she could. Only then did Felicity wring the story out of Lulu.

She listened to the tale in silence. It ended, naturally enough, on a sob.

"Do not cry, dearest. No one was injured and we shall come about."

Lulu gave a dolorous sniff. "Everyone will know. Too many people saw me. Williams and that girl from the cloakroom will tell Aunt Agnes's staff—and Miss Bliss will tell everyone else."

"Miss *Bliss?* Did she see you?"

Lulu nodded sadly. "She came into the cloakroom with another lady, someone I don't know. There was nowhere to hide. Heavens, how they stared!"

Felicity's lips tightened. Almeria Bliss was the dean's eldest daughter, a humorless young woman who never put a foot wrong—but if she had a fault, it was her taste for gossip. Miss Bliss could be counted upon to spread this tale far and wide.

"Oh, the devil fly away with Miss Bliss! This is just a silly accident that might have happened to anyone. Sit down and let me fix your hair. Are you quite certain you did not recognize the gentleman?"

Lulu sat obediently. "I did not, but he gave me his name. Stanton, or something like that."

Felicity's hands stilled. "Stanhope?"

"Yes, that was it."

Felicity returned to pulling out hairpins. Only Lulu could embarrass herself in front of the dean's daughter *and* the bishop's son, in one spectacular mishap. "Perhaps we should skip church services this week. Or wear veils."

Williams' soft knock heralded the reappearance of Lulu's silk evening gown, miraculously dried and pressed. Felicity exclaimed over Williams' skill and promised to report her excellent work to Lady DuFrayne as the stout lady's maid deftly slid Lulu into the costume and twitched the silken folds into place. Lulu's gloves were still damp, but were easily replaced with a pair borrowed from her aunt's impressive store of accessories, and the two sisters were thus, with comparative swiftness, restored to their former state. "This time," said Felicity, firmly slipping Lulu's arm through hers, "I shall escort you myself, to ensure that no further mishap befalls us."

"Us?" Lulu laughed nervously. "Generous Felicity! It is only I who suffers mishap after mishap. I suppose Aunt Agnes's guests must be wondering what became of me."

Felicity patted her sister's hand. "Perhaps the wait will have made them all the more eager to meet you."

Lulu sighed. "I was hoping they might have left by now. But I am never lucky."

As they reached the foot of the stairs, a tall man in evening clothes loomed out of the darkness. Felicity had the oddest sensation when she glimpsed him—as if a powerful attraction was pulling her toward this stranger in the dark. But no—no—it was only Gavin. She reminded herself to breathe, and ordered her skittering heart to beat normally.

"Where have you been?" he whispered. "Aunt Agnes is in a frightful quack."

"I will tell you later," she replied, also whispering. "Here—escort us in, would you? And smile, both of you, for pity's sake! All is well." She hurriedly placed Gavin between herself and Lulu.

"What a managing female you are,"

remarked Gavin. "No wonder you are still unwed."

Felicity choked back a laugh. "Must you continually remind me? I shall endeavor to correct my faults. But not tonight!"

He shook his head mournfully at her. "The leopard cannot change its spots, Felicity." But he walked them into the drawing room.

The rest of the evening proceeded without a hitch, since Lulu's adventure had frightened her into her best behavior. Apart from the knowing looks exchanged by Miss Bliss and her tittering friends, Felicity thought they managed to escape with their reputations intact—for the most part. She was relieved to see that whatever young Mr. Stanhope's message to his parents had been, he clearly had not divulged Lulu's embarrassing secret. The bishop and his wife greeted her sister with the same grave courtesy they extended to all. And only two days later, as Felicity, Lulu and Helena once again joined the DuFraynes for luncheon after a dance lesson, Lady DuFrayne announced that Mrs. Stanhope had asked her to bring Felicity and Lulu to dinner at the bishop's residence.

Lulu clapped her hands to her cheeks. "Mercy! Why would they invite us?" she exclaimed. "We have never dined with them before."

"I daresay young Stanhope wants his coat back," said Gavin.

Aunt Agnes glared at her scapegrace nephew. "Stanhope has his own residence, jackanapes, and Murdock returned the coat to him yesterday. The bishop is an old friend of mine. Quite right, quite proper, that he and Mrs. Stanhope would extend this courtesy to Lulu. Pray do not fidget, Lulu. They did as much for Felicity."

"They did," agreed Felicity. "There is

nothing to concern you, Lulu, it is only dinner. And if their son does not live with them, I daresay he will not be present."

As the sisters were donning hats and pelisses to return home, Gavin surprised Felicity by offering to escort them. Her eyes met his in the hall mirror as she tied on her hat. "Actually, I need to walk to Milsom Street. If you take Helena home, she need not accompany Lulu and me on my errand."

"Or Helena and Lulu could walk each other home while I escort you to Milsom Street."

She pulled on her gloves, no longer able to meet his eyes. It was vexing to feel nervous of him; what was the matter with her? "If you like," she said, managing to sound nonchalant despite the butterflies unaccountably fluttering in her belly. "Thank you."

"I have a particular reason for wanting to be private with you," he confessed as they descended the steps outside Aunt Agnes's front door.

"I ought to have guessed you'd have an ulterior motive," Felicity remarked. "What is it?"

He tucked her hand companionably under his elbow. The day was cold and his arm was warm. Felicity told herself that was why the gesture gave her pleasure.

"I am hoping, cousin, that you will confide in me as you used to do."

She tilted her head so she could study his face from under her hat brim, but she could not read his expression. "What a bizarre request."

"Is it? Why?"

"We are no longer children, Gavin." She laughed a little. "A woman who trusts a man generally lives to regret it."

He grinned. "I don't expect a litany of your girlish hopes and dreams, if that's what worries you."

"That's good, because I haven't any."

"I merely am curious to know your opinion of slavery."

Felicity was so astonished she nearly stumbled. She decided she must have heard him wrong. "I beg your pardon," she said at last. "It sounded exactly as if you asked my opinion of slavery."

"I did."

Felicity halted on the pavement and turned to stare at him. He returned her gaze, one eyebrow lifted.

He seemed perfectly serious. Impossible man!

"What a mad question."

"What's mad about it? It's one of the burning issues of our day."

"Gavin, for heaven's sake! You know perfectly well that respectable women don't have political opinions."

"Do they have moral opinions?"

"You're roasting me."

"No, I am not." He replaced her hand in the crook of his elbow and steered her down the hill toward Pulteney Bridge. "I want to hear your thoughts on the matter, and I don't want to sway them by disclosing my own view. Although I have probably tipped my hand by calling it a moral question."

Felicity suddenly remembered that Gavin had just spent five years in the West Indies. It gave her a queer, unsettled feeling to realize that he must have acquired first-hand knowledge of an issue that, to her, was completely abstract. She knew nothing about slavery apart from the arguments she read in newspapers, and a sermon she had once heard—the thrust of which, as she cudgeled her brain to recall it, had been more about charity, kindness, and duty, than a thundering denunciation of the practice. After all, slavery was in the Bible, where it seemed to be dealt with matter-of-factly as an unalterable condition of human life.

"I defer to you," she said at last. "You clearly have a better-informed point of view than I am ever likely to have. You are a man of the world; I am a Bath miss. You have seen with your own eyes what I have only read about."

"You have no opinion of your own, then?"

"On this subject, no."

"You disappoint me."

Felicity glanced up into his face again and was stung by his expression. "Gavin," she said, exasperated. "Do you not see how presumptuous it would be, for me to put forward an opinion of my own when I am obviously ill-informed, and you are not? It is unhandsome of you to ask me to expose my ignorance, since I have already acknowledged it."

"Then you do have an opinion."

"Every thinking person must have an opinion on such a... such a *fraught* subject. If you must know, the thought of slavery lowers my spirits. And as there is nothing whatsoever I can do about it, I do not often think about it. There! Am I shallow, or merely practical?"

He smiled. "You are honest. And now you are cross with me."

She bit her lip. "A little. I daresay you are about to tell me why you so rudely put me on the spot. It can't have been merely to amuse yourself at my expense."

They had reached the bustle surrounding the shops on the bridge, so Gavin did not answer her until they had threaded their way through the throng of people and were headed toward Milsom Street.

"You are correct," he said at last, "that my question was not prompted by idle curiosity, nor a desire to make you appear foolish."

"Well, that's something," said Felicity.

He laughed. "What if I told you there was something you could do?"

"About slavery?" she exclaimed. "I'd say you were daft."

"Not slavery itself," he admitted. "That's perhaps a little beyond your powers."

"I daresay!"

"But Felicity, you might be able to help one or two people." His voice had dropped into a serious tone. She glanced doubtfully at his face again, and saw that his expression was intent and sober. "Sixty-seven people, to be exact. Sixty-seven human souls who are presently trapped in Barbados, awaiting rescue."

Felicity raised one gloved hand to stop him. "No more," she said firmly. "This is not a discussion we can have on Milsom Street. Have you ever had a Bath bun?"

"Many times."

"But not in Bath. Come! We will sit and speak to each other face-to-face, like civilized creatures, and you will tell me whatever tale is presently burning in your brain."

## Chapter Six

The cheerful, bustling tea shop was full of light from the large windows that fronted the street. It was so very English, with its linens and porcelain and the fragrance of tea, it was difficult for Felicity to transport herself mentally to the sweltering sugar cane fields Gavin described. He spoke of the sprawling wooden house his father and he had shared, with wide verandas and tall windows to catch the breeze, and she almost laughed picturing her unlikable Uncle Monty in such exotic surroundings.

She regarded Gavin over the rim of her teacup. "Did the warm climate agree with your father?"

"It did, to my surprise. Mayhap the heat matched his temper."

"I was rather astonished when you followed him out there. When last I knew you, you and he were not on good terms."

"We never were," said Gavin. "But I was his heir, so he asked me to interest myself in the plantation. It seemed a reasonable request, and I am not entirely blind to family duty, so I went. I thought I might like the islands as much as he did. Alas, I did not. It became yet another point of friction between us." His expression turned wry.

"Were you hoping that my shocking lack of filial affection was something I would outgrow?"

"Yes," she said. "But for your sake, not your father's. No one seemed to care much for him. Was he really as impossible as he appeared to be? If so, I am sorry for it."

"Thank you. He was."

The tea room swirled with waiters delivering steaming pots and salvers of Bath buns to tables all around them. Gavin stared moodily at his plate. "Is there fruit in this thing? I can't abide cake with fruit."

"No fruit, but a lump of sugar in the center."

He picked up his bun and paused, glancing across the table at his companion. "You may be interested to learn that a man does not tire of sugar, however intimately he lives with it. It's fine stuff, isn't it? Look at it, sparkling so prettily on top of this otherwise undistinguished-looking bap."

"Beautiful," she agreed, her eyes twinkling.

"I daresay you've never given a thought to the backbreaking labor it takes to produce these dainty crystals."

"No. How should I?" She swallowed another sip of tea. "Although I'm sure the process is very interesting, of course."

"It is," he said. "Provided someone else is doing the work."

"Ah," she said, quirking an eyebrow. "Which brings us back, no doubt, to the topic of slavery."

"Yes." Gavin helped himself liberally to the butter, his lips tightening into a thin line. She had never seen him look so grim. "You were reluctant to divulge your opinion on the matter, but now that I have choked it out of you I shall readily give you mine. It's a beastly practice, and a stain on every nation that permits it."

Well. That was certainly a definitive statement. What had he seen in the West Indies, to convince him so utterly? The tea suddenly seemed less flavorful than it had been a moment ago. She set down her cup and placed her hands in her lap. "I am sorry to hear that," she said quietly. "I have read tales that kept me awake at night, but one naturally hopes that the more lurid stories are untrue. Or at least exaggerated, since the object of such stories is to make an argument. Are there not..." She hesitated. "Is it not possible to treat people well, regardless of their status? Surely not every owner—"

"Every owner," said Gavin vehemently. "Some are worse than others, but it is not possible to deprive a man of liberty, of the power to control his own destiny, of the free will bestowed upon him by his Creator, without wronging him. These people have been deeply wronged, every one of them." He smiled, it seemed, with an effort. "But I have run ahead of my tale."

"Some of the story I can easily surmise. Uncle Monty obviously employed slaves on his sugar plantation, and you came to abhor it. But why did he do it?"

He had taken a bite of his bun and had to swallow before he could reply. "To make money, my innocent." He stirred his tea. "A sugar plantation requires a large and specialized work force, laboring around the clock. It can't be run profitably if the workers must be *paid.*"

Felicity's expression must have communicated her feelings; Gavin uttered a short bark of mirthless laughter. "Exactly. In addition, although some of the work is not particularly bad—no worse than regular farming—much of it is so difficult, so exhausting, that no one would do it if not forced. Oppressive heat, burning sun, backbreaking labor, snakes that crawl and insects that swarm, many that suck blood—"

"Pray stop." Felicity held up one hand and closed her eyes in pain. "I believe you. I do not require a detailed picture."

"Very well. I confess, much to my shame, that it was only when my father's health failed and I stepped into a management role that I comprehended the enormity..." He fell silent for a moment, frowning into his cup. "At any rate, I became aware simultaneously that trafficking in human flesh was an unmitigated evil, and that my father's newfound fortune would have been impossible to acquire without it." His eyes met hers, glinting with dark amusement. "A dilemma."

"Dear me," said Felicity faintly. "What did you do?"

"There was little I could do while my father lived. I was able to mitigate the harshness of their treatment, but had no power to restore their freedom—or anything like it—until he passed. When he fell ill, I put out a few discreet inquiries and found a fellowship of Quakers in Bridgetown led by an abolitionist named Goodwin. He assisted me with the legalities and logistics of securing the freedom of several hundred people. It proved to be no easy task. But by the time my father left this earth, I had everything in order and was able to set them free."

"That is wonderful!" she exclaimed.

He gave her a rueful smile. "Thank you, but unfortunately the tale does not end there. As I already mentioned, a sugar plantation cannot run itself. It requires an ample supply of cheap labor. I soon learned that if I were to sell my land—which I intended to do as quickly as possible—either the human property would need to be included in the sale, or I must sell the land very cheaply indeed, to enable the purchaser to staff the place with—what else? More slaves."

He was trying to speak lightly, but Felicity knew him well. The strain around his eyes and the tension in his shoulders informed her that the situation had grieved him. Impulsively she reached across the table and laid her hand on his sleeve. "You cannot cure all the ills of the world," she said.

"Not alone." He gave her another crooked smile. "But man is a vain creature, Felicity. This man is, at any rate. It hurt my pride to discover how limited my powers were. I could set my own people free, but could not free every slave in Barbados. I was trying to empty the ocean with a teaspoon."

A waiter came by to replenish their tea. Felicity quickly withdrew her hand, blushing a little. She had been so focused on their conversation, for a moment she had forgotten where they were.

"But you did what you could. You accomplished the task that was set before you. You set them free, didn't you, Gavin? The people your father had—had owned." The word was distasteful to utter.

"Most of them. Believe it or not, several declined my offer."

She gasped. "Why?"

"I suppose because a life in bondage was the only life they knew. Human nature is a peculiar thing. There are those who are so fearful of the unknown that they cling to a life of hardship rather than face change. And, admittedly, life as a freedman in Barbados is not necessarily easy. To be turned loose in the world with no education, no home, no friends waiting to embrace and support you—such a fate is, perhaps, only for the young and strong. Two who

73

told me they would rather be sold with the plantation were elderly, and one was blind and had spent her entire life there. She feared—perhaps rightly—that there would be no life for her in Bridgeport, where her skill at sugar scraping would be worthless. Even if you dream of freedom all your life, you might shrink from it when it arrives. Freedom can bring fearsome changes."

Felicity stared out the window, trying to fathom it. A boy in a blue apron ran by. Carriages passed. Somewhere, a horse neighed. Three young girls carrying muffs walked past the window, giggling. It all seemed so normal and cheerful, so completely ordinary.

"What a sheltered life I have led," she whispered.

Gavin lifted his cup in a salute. "And long may you live it," he said. "I have no wish to drag you into the midst of the world's troubles." He drank, then set his cup down and refilled it. "I have not finished my story."

She sighed, shaking her head. "I hope it has a happy ending."

He smiled. "Certainly. For in the end, I sold the plantation and purchased freedom for three hundred and sixteen people. I wish it had been more, but I'm grateful I had the means to do that much."

"It is wonderful," said Felicity staunchly. "Truly, Gavin, it is wonderful. Although it is a great pity you had to sell the land to do it. I think you saw a great wrong, and did what you could to right it. That is all any of us can do. If the new owner runs the plantation with slaves, you must not reproach yourself. That is on his conscience, not yours."

"Thank you, but in the end, I could not bring myself to allow it." The gleam of humor returned to his eyes. "Who do you think purchased my plantation?"

"I've no idea."

"Friend Goodwin."

Felicity was startled, but delighted. "No!"

He grinned. "I had to cut the price considerably, but I would have had to cut it regardless, to sell it without slaves. He wanted to experiment with running a plantation cooperatively, as he called it—manning it with freedmen who knew the work, but letting them share in the profits. He also intends to set up a school on the property, bless him. Several of his like-minded friends went in on the venture, and I believe he took up a subscription for the rest of the funds. And there you have it."

"Did the people you freed stay on Monty's plantation after all, then?"

"Many did, including, of course, the few who declined their legal freedom. It was a great relief to me to know that they would be slaves in name only, living there and working for the abolitionists. I daresay they'll quickly embrace the notion of freedom, once they put a toe in the water and nothing bites them."

"But not all stayed, after Mr. Goodwin purchased it?"

He shook his head. "By no means. Some hated the place so much, they wouldn't stay an instant longer than was necessary. Some had better prospects elsewhere, or wanted to try their hand at working in town, or going to sea." He lifted his teacup again, inhaling the fragrant steam, then sighed. "Which left sixty-seven."

"Ah." Felicity cocked her head, regarding him curiously. "You did mention sixty-seven."

"I hope that, by this time, the actual number is somewhat lower. But when I left Barbados, I had sixty-seven dependents holed up in various rooms near the port in Bridgetown, waiting for passage to England—passage that I promised to arrange. If some have found suitable situations in Barbados by now, that's well and good. But I dare not assume it. I brought my manservant, David, with me, but sixty-seven I left behind—with only my word to cling to."

Felicity frowned. "You promised them passage to England? Did you promise them employment here as well?"

"No," he admitted. "I was not as rash as that. But this group, facing a new life, desired to try their luck in a land where the color of their skin would not automatically condemn them to a life of bondage. And I felt certain I could enlist Aunt Agnes's help in getting them here, once I explained the situation to her."

Felicity nearly choked on her tea. She set her cup down with great care, then stared very hard at Gavin. "You thought *Aunt Agnes* would purchase passage for all these people?"

He nodded glumly. "I believed it all the way across the sea. Believed it, in fact, until I actually sat down with her."

Felicity pressed one hand to her cheek, horrified. "Did you *ask* her?"

"No."

"Thank heaven! Gavin, she only just agreed to bring Lulu out. Do you know what a Season in London costs? We couldn't possibly approach her for more—"

"I didn't," he almost snapped. "Not out of consideration for her purse—which is larger than you, perhaps, realize—but because I saw at once how difficult it would be for her to imagine their plight. But Felicity, I know these people." He leaned across the table toward her, his expression urgent. "They are my responsibility, as much as if they were members of my family. It is I who put

76

them in this position. And I gave them my word."

"Why, then, you must honor it. You must shoulder the cost. You sold your land."

"I did, but not at the profit I would have made—ah, there is no use in thinking of that. I do not regret that decision." His mouth quirked ruefully again. "It is what I did with the money that I regret." Something in her expression caused him to lift a hand in protest. "Nothing bacon-brained, I promise you! Merely... inconvenient. Under the circumstances." He studied her face. "I daresay you know little about investments."

"Naturally not. Women do not handle money."

"Suffice it to say, then, that the longer you agree to tie your money up, the better return you can secure. I received considerably less for my land than I might have, so it behooved me to invest the funds wisely. I did so. But now I cannot touch the principal for at least three years. And the first income payment will not arrive until twelve months after I signed the contract."

"Gracious! How will you live?"

He laughed. "I have plenty of pocket change, Cousin, never fear. But passage to England from Barbados for sixty-seven people is beyond my means."

Felicity looked askance at him. "You said I could help. You must have been joking."

Gavin's expression sobered. "I believe you could, but I don't know if you will."

"What on earth—"

"Felicity, my need is pressing. I put it to you: What would you do, were you in my shoes? I have inherited the DuFrayne baronetcy, but not the DuFrayne fortune. Do you not think, as I do, that it is my aunt's duty to assist me?"

"No, Gavin, I do not. You asked me to be

frank with you. I understand your position and I sympathize with it, but no. Your quarrel is with your late uncle, Sir Jasper, not with Aunt Agnes. You have no more right to hang on her sleeve than..." She choked, then looked away. "Than I do."

Silence fell. Gavin lifted an eyebrow and regarded her steadily. Drat the man!

"I suppose," she said stiffly, "that you will try to convince me to relinquish my own claims on Aunt Agnes's purse. You will tell me Lulu is not ready, and we would do better to wait a year before bringing her out."

"I did not say so."

"But you think it."

To her surprise, he chuckled. "Do not tempt me, Felicity. I would love to tell you exactly that, but I will not repay your frankness with a falsehood. I think Lulu will be as ready by this spring as she will ever be. So could you postpone her debut? Should you? That is a question only you and Aunt Agnes can answer."

Exasperated, Felicity glared at him. "Why don't you rail at me and tell me I am selfish and shallow?"

"Because you are not."

"I am! I have no desire to approach Aunt Agnes and ask her to postpone Lulu's debut, merely so she can rescue your suffering friends instead."

"Then why are you proposing it?"

"I am not proposing it! Quite the opposite. I am telling you I don't want to do it, and you shouldn't ask it of me."

"Very well. I shan't ask it of you. You're quite right; it was wrong of me to depend on Aunt Agnes—or you, for that matter. I have gotten myself into this scrape. I must get myself out."

This was precisely her own position. How

aggravating that hearing it stated in Gavin's calm voice somehow made her doubt herself.

Felicity bit her lip, irresolute. "Naturally, I wish I could help. Do you suppose we could... take up a subscription? I could write letters..." Her voice trailed off. Her imagination failed her as she tried to imagine what such a letter might say. "Oh dear."

Gavin's lips twitched. "Do you have a large circle of wealthy friends, Felicity? Friends, I need hardly point out, who are unacquainted with our aunt?"

Felicity's eyes widened with dismay. "Gracious me. Everyone I send a letter to will tell Aunt Agnes."

Their eyes met over the table for one pregnant moment as they imagined Aunt Agnes's reaction, and suddenly they both burst out laughing.

Felicity was guiltily aware of the curious faces turned toward them, and tried to stifle her laughter in her serviette. "Well," she managed to gasp, "That bird will not fly."

"Let's think of something else," suggested Gavin, picking up his hat. "While I walk you up Milsom Street."

A waiter materialized behind her chair and assisted her to rise. Felicity shook out the folds of her pelisse and stepped to take Gavin's arm. "Very well," she said equably as they left the shop. "We must think of something else. Because I simply can't postpone Lulu's Season. It wouldn't be fair, after promising her."

"No," he agreed. "Although I appreciate your suggesting it."

"I am not suggesting it!"

His eyes gleamed down at her. "Then why do you keep bringing it up?"

## Chapter Seven

Nora tucked the last comb into Lulu's artfully-arranged mop of curls and stepped back to gauge the effect. She could not step far back, because the bedchamber was small to begin with and was, at the moment, a trifle overcrowded. Lulu was seated on the worn tuffet before their mother's vanity mirror. Mama stood at the back of the room looking over Nora's shoulder, and Felicity stood beside them, supervising.

"It is beautiful, Nora, truly," said Felicity. "Williams herself could not do better."

"Is it fashionable?" asked Nora. "I copied it from *La Belle Assemblee*."

"Fashionable, and becoming as well."

"Very pretty," said Mama.

Lulu beamed. "I scarcely recognize myself."

Felicity laughed. "I'd know you anywhere. Stand up, Lulu, so we can lace you into the gown."

Lulu thought proudly that Felicity's eye for fashion, Nora's talent for hairdressing and hat-trimming, and Mama's skill with a needle, more than made up for the household's lack of a lady's maid. Not that she knew the first thing about it, of course. Still, by the time her mother and sisters were done with her, Lulu was fetchingly arrayed in a slightly-altered version of one of Felicity's dinner dresses from her first season. She looked rather sweet, she thought hopefully, stealing a glance at her reflection as Felicity and Mama smoothed her skirts and tugged the bodice into place and Nora tied her sash.

Not that it mattered, she reminded herself. Felicity had promised her over and over that Oliver Stanhope would likely *not* be present tonight. Which was the only thing enabling her to face dinner with the bishop and his wife with any degree of poise. He won't be there, she told herself firmly. He won't be there. Nothing to worry about; nothing to get excited about; Oliver Stanhope had his own residence and there was no earthly reason why his parents would include him in this simple invitation to Lady DuFrayne to bring Felicity and Lulu to dinner. Just a simple dinner. And probably whist would follow—according to Felicity, who had reason to know. A perfectly boring, pleasant evening awaited her. Mere practice. Tonight was not important at all.

The Stanhopes lived in an imposing stone manse past Sydney Gardens, well uphill of Laura Place, so they took Aunt Agnes's carriage. A light snow was falling and the pavement crunched beneath her slippers as the party alighted and approached the bishop's residence. As she climbed the low stone steps she whispered *it's only dinner, it's only dinner* under her breath like a mantra. Felicity overheard her and squeezed her gloved hand. Lulu gave her sister a shaky smile and subsided into silence as the door swung open before them and a butler divested the party of their cloaks. She still felt unaccountably frightened, as if she were about to walk onto a stage without knowing her lines. Gavin and Felicity exchanged quizzical glances over her head, but she paid them no mind; it was time to concentrate.

All was a blur as she followed Aunt Agnes and Gavin into the drawing room and made her curtsey to the Stanhopes, but her hammering heart subsided into something like a normal rhythm when she perceived that none of the faces in the room belonged to Oliver Stanhope— although two young men were present whom she did not know. Mrs. Stanhope introduced them as her eldest son, James, who had come from his parsonage in the midlands to spend Christmas with his parents, and their youngest son, Charles, who was also following his father's footsteps into the clergy.

James was a tall, stoop-shouldered man probably ten years her senior. Charles appeared close to her own age, but had the thin frame and saintly demeanor of an ascetic. Neither could hold a candle to their brother Oliver, thought Lulu— then quickly banished the thought, biting her lip, as Mrs. Stanhope turned to include her other guests in the conversation. "Of course you know Dean Bliss and Mrs. Bliss," she was saying, "and their daughter, Almeria."

Lulu's composure slipped. She gawked in dismay at Dean and Mrs. Bliss and their daughter, Almeria. Their expressions were so frosty that she instantly knew Almeria had told them the story of finding her in the ladies' cloakroom, soaked and shivering and wrapped in a gentleman's coat. Miss Bliss's features were rigid with amused contempt even as she murmured a greeting to the Pennington sisters. Worse—Mrs. Bliss was looking very grave, and her bow to Lulu was so small that it was hazardously close to a cut. Lulu's heart sank. She curtseyed and stammered some incoherent greeting, but she hardly knew what she said.

Felicity swiftly stepped up to rescue her, shaking the dean's hand and remarking easily on the weather in her friendly way—but Almeria's eyes remained on Lulu, her supercilious smile redolent of disdain. Lulu, miserable, dropped her eyes to the floor and studied the carpet, wishing she could crawl beneath it.

Behind her, the door opened. "And here at last is our middle son!" said Mrs. Stanhope. "Oliver, step forward and meet Lady DuFrayne, Sir Gavin DuFrayne, and the Pennington sisters."

Lulu, covered with confusion, felt a hot blush climbing up her neck. She dared not lift her gaze as Oliver Stanhope was introduced to Aunt Agnes, then Gavin, then Felicity. But her turn came at last and she was forced to look into Mr. Stanhope's face and say something. She cast an imploring glance into his eyes and found them smiling into hers. And then—he winked! It was barely perceptible, but she caught it, and almost gasped with relief. Her heart warmed as she realized that, unlike Miss Bliss, he had definitely kept her secret. His mother introduced them with not a flicker of consciousness; she clearly had no clue that they had met before. Lulu curtseyed gratefully and murmured something polite, unable to care anymore what the Bliss family thought of her.

She followed Felicity to a narrow bench upholstered in horsehair and perched beside her sister, prepared to copy her more experienced, confident sibling as closely as possible. If she patterned her behavior on Felicity's, she thought, she could not go wrong. The bishop, meanwhile, clapped Oliver on his shoulder and asked, "How long did it take you to get here, my boy?"

"Twenty-six minutes," said Oliver, with a great air of satisfaction.

Mrs. Stanhope exclaimed at that, then

turned to explain to the room at large. "Oliver has purchased a house, and we are so pleased that he found something suitable. It will be very pleasant to have him near us, since our other boys must go where their calling sends them."

Amid the congratulations, Felicity asked, "How did you settle on Bath, Mr. Stanhope? Many of the gentlemen I meet in London have a sad view of our town, and think it fit only for dowagers and slowtops." She softened the impertinence of her question with a smile.

Mr. Stanhope returned her smile. "I have always thought Bath beautiful," he said simply, choosing a seat across from the Pennington sisters. "And having spent some years in Yorkshire, I have a new appreciation for a tamer landscape and milder climate."

"Are you actually in town, then?"

"Not quite. It is a country house, but not far removed from here." He grinned. "I won't deceive you, Miss Pennington; I can make the trip in twenty-six minutes, but it takes longer for most people."

Miss Bliss raised her hands and rolled her eyes toward heaven. "Oliver's fast horses!" she exclaimed, sinking onto the sofa beside him. "I would shake with fear to ride any one of them."

Lulu felt Felicity stiffen beside her, but wasn't sure why. Mr. Stanhope, meanwhile, gave Almeria a perfunctory smile and returned his attention to Felicity and Lulu. "I am fond of fast horses," he admitted, "but I am not one of those neck-or-nothing chaps."

Gavin started to laugh and turned it into a cough. "Very wise," he said at last.

The conversation ebbed and flowed, centering on plans for Christmas, James Stanhope's duties at his new parish, the progress of young Charles's studies, the weather, and other such topics. Lulu was content to sit happily and smile, basking in Mr. Stanhope's presence— now that the most pressing of her fears had been laid to rest.

Beside her, Lulu seemed lost in a beatific reverie. Felicity could not help but perceive that her sister's gaze rested frequently on Oliver Stanhope, and that her dreamy smile intensified each time it did. Vexing child! Had she formed a *tendre* for the man already—and was she determined to expose it to the world? Under the circumstances, it was impossible to pull her sister aside or have any sort of private word with her.

Meanwhile, Almeria Bliss was doing her utmost to signal to the Pennington sisters that she had staked a claim on Mr. Stanhope herself. And Lulu, bless her, saw none of it. Felicity was acutely aware of Gavin's intense enjoyment of the situation, since he leaned against the mantelpiece nearby, very much at his ease, and occasionally hiding a grin behind his hand. It made her cross. From the instant Miss Bliss claimed the seat beside 'Oliver' and called him by his Christian name, the tilt of her head and the way she leaned her body toward his every time she spoke or laughed was meant to convey a message. Felicity received the message quite clearly. Lulu, however, seemed oblivious.

She supposed, reluctantly, that she might have found the situation as amusing as Gavin did—had it been anyone other than Lulu who was the unwitting target of Miss Bliss's pointed arrows. As each well-aimed shaft whistled past Lulu's unsuspecting head, Felicity found it more and more difficult to keep her own smile pinned securely in place. It was a relief when the party was called in to dinner.

Dinner, however, was a tedious affair. The Stanhopes were a pleasant couple, but quiet and humorless. Felicity was placed beside James Stanhope and soon found that nothing more was required of her than a polite nod or smile from time to time. He dominated the conversation with detailed descriptions of his parish, his new parsonage, and the surrounding village. All she need do was murmur, "Really?" or "How nice," at intervals.

Ten minutes of young Rev. Stanhope's company was enough to convince her that he was not the man for Lulu. Charles might be a better match, were he not so callow—and scholarly—and timid. Oliver, however, she had liked at once. It tickled her to discover that the paragon described to her in such glowing terms by Lulu was a perfectly ordinary gentleman in his mid-twenties, rather short, with a square, solid build and kind eyes. When he bowed to Lulu, Felicity perceived what had bewitched her sister; he really did have a delightful, good-humored smile, and to his credit he clearly had breathed not a word of Lulu's escapade to any of his family. Overall, she was inclined to approve of him.

Except that he was probably not on offer in the marriage-market. Poor Lulu!

And poor Oliver, she thought. Although it was none of her affair, of course. She had never been a particular friend of Miss Bliss, but she had never disliked her before this evening. Now she perceived streaks of jealousy and possessiveness in her, faults that, when coupled with her taste for sensational gossip, might render her future husband's life uncomfortable— whoever that man might be.

Miss Bliss clearly intended her future husband to be Oliver Stanhope. And judging by the indulgent smiles of both Mrs. Stanhope and Mrs. Bliss, Almeria's chances of securing the match were good. Ah, well. Lulu had not yet seen the world. There were other men in it, and she would soon forget Mr. Stanhope.

Now if only it were possible to catch Lulu's eye, and signal her to stop smiling at him!

Oliver was afraid it might be a dull evening for the lively Pennington sisters. He loved his family, naturally, but they were a somber lot. He himself had never quite fit in, despite many attempts over the years to quell his tendency toward levity.

His heart sank as he entered the drawing room and saw that three game tables had been set up for whist. Whist! The very name of the game meant 'be quiet.' He suppressed a sigh and managed to smile and hold Almeria's chair for her as she claimed him for her partner, archly commenting that, "Oliver and I are so accustomed to partnering each other, I declare I do not know how to play with anyone else!" He wished she would not crowd him so, but she seemed edgy and anxious tonight for some reason. He must learn to bear her moods with equanimity, he reminded himself, and gave her another smile as he sat across from her.

To his right, Sir Gavin was seating Lucille Pennington, who looked even more nervous than Almeria. She stammered her thanks to Sir Gavin and cast an apologetic look up at him. "I'm afraid I'm not very good at whist," she confessed.

"Never mind," said Sir Gavin, coming

round to take the last chair at their small table. "I'll kick you under the table from time to time, to help you with your play."

Miss Lulu giggled, but Almeria looked shocked. Sir Gavin smiled at her. "I am joking, Miss Bliss," he said. "Forgive me."

"Ah." Almeria gave an unconvincing little laugh. "Of course. It would be cheating, as I'm sure you know, to signal your partner in any way."

"Painful, too," Lulu remarked. "Although I would try to bear it if it helped us win."

Oliver laughed. "Are you such a cutthroat competitor, Miss Lulu?"

Her blue eyes sparkled. "Yes, I am. Isn't it dreadful? If we were playing lottery instead of whist, I would vanquish you all, and show no mercy. I would leave you moaning on the carpet without a backward look."

"Then I do not despair," said Sir Gavin. "Between my skill and your killer instincts, we may play creditably after all."

At the tables, cards were dealt and the customary quiet of whist, broken only by desultory conversation, set in.

Except, that is, at Oliver's table.

Miss Pennington wiggled, bounced in her chair, and exclaimed—under her breath, to be sure—at every hand she was dealt and every play that was made. "Ha!" she would cry as she took a trick, eyes sparkling. "Noooo," she would moan as her fortunes fell. Oliver and Sir Gavin did not even try to keep their gravity. They laughed outright as Miss Lulu repeatedly broke the rules of silence, seeming unable to contain herself.

"You see how it is," she remarked despairingly as the cards were shuffled at the end of the first rubber. "I am hopeless at whist."

Oliver smiled. "But I have never seen a

player enjoy herself more."

She nodded earnestly. "That is precisely the problem. I *love* to play at cards. My sisters draw straws to decide who must partner me, because I ruin the game for whoever draws the short straw."

Sir Gavin's eyes twinkled. "What a terrible spy you would be, Lulu. You cannot keep a secret."

"Oh! I can if it's important." Her curls bounced as she waxed indignant. "I might make a wonderful spy. I am not afraid of anything." She bit her lip. "Except dinner parties."

Sir Gavin and Oliver burst out laughing. To her credit, Miss Lulu laughed as well, although she turned a little pink. "We all have our weak spots," she declared, lifting her chin.

"Yes," said Sir Gavin. "And although you and I lost, the score was very close. With a little luck, we shall come about."

They did, in fact, win the next rubber, largely due to the luck of the draw. Lulu Pennington, anyone could see, tried manfully to suppress her emotions, but her flushed cheeks and bright eyes frequently gave her away, and Oliver could not resist teasing her about it. To his delight, she did not take offense, but riposted with spirit. He could never remember enjoying whist so much—or, for that matter, laughing so hard—at any of his parents' social gatherings.

At the end of the rubber, as Sir Gavin shuffled the deck, Oliver became guiltily aware that their noise had drawn the attention of the other players in the room. Curious glances, and a few annoyed ones, were being directed at his table. And then—Almeria! Good heavens. He had completely forgotten about Almeria. They were playing as partners, but Oliver's whole attention had been focused on the entrancing Miss Lulu.

Almeria sat upright in her chair, rigid with disapproval, or anger, or wounded feelings— really, he hardly knew what. She was never easy to read. He suddenly realized she had not once joined in the laughter and conversation he'd been enjoying so much.

He tried to include her with a smile. "You are much better behaved than we are, Almeria."

"I own, I do not understand how we can call our game 'whist' unless we follow the rules." She played a card with a decided snap. "It is difficult to note which cards have been played, with so much distraction."

Her waspish tone startled him. Beside him, Miss Lulu clapped her hands to her cheeks, looking distressed. "I am so sorry—" she began, but Sir Gavin interrupted her.

"We three are a rowdy lot, Miss Bliss," he said, sounding apologetic. "I daresay Miss Pennington would be happy to change places with you, if you like. She's playing with Rev. Stanhope, your father, and Mrs. Stanhope. They seem far more focused on the game than Felicity will ever be." He leaned toward Almeria in a confidential manner. "I have played whist with her before, and she's as poor a player as Lulu here."

"She is not!" cried Miss Lulu—which surprised another laugh out of Oliver.

His laugh seemed to make up Almeria's mind. Two spots of color appeared high on her cheekbones. She slapped her cards face-down on the table and pushed back her chair, not waiting for either of the men to assist her. "An excellent suggestion," she said angrily. Oliver and Sir Gavin quickly rose as she did, and Oliver hastened to escort her to his mother's table and effect the change of partners. He could not remember seeing Almeria this cross, and wondered at it. It seemed a slight, even paltry, cause to elicit so much fury.

He hesitated after seating her. Should he apologize? If so—for what? He discovered that her peevishness had sparked an answering irritation in him, and, as tight-lipped as she, bowed to her in silence. Then he returned to his own table with Felicity Pennington on his arm. He began to seat her where Almeria had been.

"Oh, no you don't," said Sir Gavin, holding up one hand as if to stop him. "I have suffered enough, Stanhope. *You* partner Lulu for a while."

The sisters cried out at this rudeness, laughing, but the two girls did change places so that Lucille Pennington sat across from Oliver, and Miss Pennington partnered Sir Gavin.

"Well? Do not keep me in suspense," remarked Miss Pennington, expertly reshuffling the deck. "What was all that about?"

"All what about?" asked Sir Gavin.

She paused and gave him a severe look, then began to deal. "That little maneuver Mr. Stanhope executed just now. Pray do not think I am ungrateful—"

"Oh, were you bored?" enquired Sir Gavin. "How rag-mannered of you to disclose it."

Miss Pennington choked back a laugh. "I was not bored, you unconscionable wretch. I merely meant—"

"You were expiring of curiosity."

"Naturally." She calmly finished the deal. "I wondered what game was being played at this table."

Oliver placed his hand over his heart. "Whist, ma'am, upon my honor."

Miss Pennington looked slyly through her lashes, first at him, then at Sir Gavin. "You were having far too much fun to be playing whist."

Oliver saw that his new partner was blushing and biting her lip. He gave her what he hoped was a reassuring smile. "I daresay any game, even whist, is entertaining when played with Miss Lucille Pennington."

At that, Miss Lulu raised shining eyes to his face and bestowed a blinding smile on him that nearly took his breath away. For a moment, he forgot where he was. Beside him, Sir Gavin cleared his throat. "Your play, Stanhope."

Oliver blinked. "Sorry." He played a card at random, and lost the trick. It didn't seem to matter much. He'd collected his wits by the time the play returned to him, but both he and Miss Lulu played atrociously throughout the rubber and lost rather badly.

"Like taking candy from a baby," remarked Miss Pennington, totting up the score. "What a pity we are not playing silver-loo."

The party broke up soon after that, the card tables were whisked away, and tea arrived. Oliver, feeling a pang of remorse, sought out Almeria.

"I have brought you a cup with lemon," he said, presenting it to her with a smile. "I know your preferences well, do I not?"

She returned his smile, seemingly with an effort, and thanked him. He seated himself in the chair nearest to her and addressed her in a low tone. "I am sorry our noise drove you away. Are you feeling quite the thing?"

"Just a touch of the megrims, perhaps," she said. The tightness around her mouth did not lessen. "You know I am prone to headaches, Oliver."

"Perhaps the tea will help."

"Perhaps." A short bark of bitter laughter escaped her. "And I shall feel better yet when the Penningtons depart. I cannot like those girls, try as I might."

Oliver felt surprised. "May I ask why? They

seem perfectly respectable, good-humored young women. And I understand that Lady DuFrayne is a pillar of the community. My father tells me she is very generous to the church."

Almeria hunched a shoulder pettishly. "Oh, I daresay Lady DuFrayne is everything admirable—although you must own, she can be excessively rude."

"I do not know her well."

"Naturally not." Almeria sipped her tea. "But when you have been in Bath a while, you shall. Believe me, that woman is inescapable."

Definitely megrims, Oliver decided. He had seldom heard Almeria sound so sulky. "The Penningtons are her brother's children, I believe?"

"Correct. And Miss Pennington will be exactly like her aunt in forty years! So much assurance! I never met a more forward young woman. She has an opinion about everything, and never hesitates to voice it. Everyone says she is clever, but I think that sort of wit is unbecoming in a female. And as for Miss Lulu—!" Almeria rolled her eyes expressively, but clamped her lips as if stopping herself from saying too much.

Oliver frowned. "Miss Lucille Pennington is not unbecomingly forward, surely? My impression is that she is rather shy."

"Ah. Yes? Appearances can be deceptive." Almeria's eyes lit with malicious amusement. "Tonight, I thought her behavior merely immature. So little self-control! But I have seen her in worse scrapes than you will easily believe." She leaned an elbow on the arm of her chair and inclined her body closer to him, lowering her voice. "Do you know where I found her, on the very evening when Lady DuFrayne first brought her to the notice of her friends? You will never guess."

Oliver's frown deepened, but Almeria did not seem to notice. She cast a surreptitious glance around the room, then leaned closer to him, smiling. "I encountered Miss Lulu in the ladies' cloakroom, wrapped in a gentleman's coat—not an overcoat, mind you, but his evening coat! And wet to the skin! When I discovered her, you cannot imagine the state she was in—and how strange and guilty her expression, I cannot describe! She looked ready to sink—could not meet my eyes—and had not a single word to say to me. Well, for *that* I cannot blame her. Indeed, what might she have said? I was never more astonished. The night of her debut! What could account for it, do you think? What sort of scrape could she possibly have been in? Soaked to the skin, and evidently in the company of a man—a man who had, perforce, to strip off his own coat to lend her a little modesty! *Now* what think you of your bashful Miss Lulu? I can find no innocent construction to put on such a sight."

"Really?" he said, hanging onto his temper with both hands. "I find it difficult to invent a sinister interpretation of that scene. I would assume a perfectly innocent mishap had occurred. Something unlucky, rather than scandalous."

Almeria's laugh was like the tinkling of little bells. For the first time, it failed to charm him. "Oh, Oliver, you are too good for this world!"

Anger licked through him, but he was spared the necessity of answering because his mother called out to him to come and bid farewell to their guests. Lady DuFrayne had grown tired, and the party was ending. In the hubbub of shaking hands and wishing everyone a good night, Oliver seized a chance to help Almeria with her cloak. As she smiled her thanks, he leaned in to her and said, as pleasantly as he could, "Did you happen to notice the cut and color of the gentleman's coat Miss Lucille Pennington borrowed?"

She looked confused. "You mean—the night when I discovered her in the cloakroom? No. No, I did not particularly mark it. Why?"

He bowed, then fingered one of his lapels and arched a brow at her. "Why, nothing," he said. "But that explains why you did not recognize the coat when you saw it again this evening. Good night, Almeria."

## Chapter Eight

The weather turned bitterly cold, and although it did not snow a hard frost seemed to dust the golden stone of Bath with powdered sugar. As December closed in, there were not enough hours of sunshine to melt the frost entirely, and within a few days the city glittered like a sugar plum. Felicity's breath steamed as she strode briskly from Henrietta Street to Laura Place. She did not mind the cold; the walk was short and the morning beautiful.

As she crossed Great Pulteney Street, she was surprised to see Gavin approaching from her left. He touched his hat brim when he saw her, so she waited for him when she reached the pavement.

"Good morrow, Cousin," he said, rubbing his gloved hands together. "Brrr! I'd forgotten what winter feels like."

She laughed at him. "Do you wish now that you'd stayed in Barbados?"

"That, never," he said firmly. "Was I complaining? I ought, instead, to have told you how refreshed I feel by the briskness of the air."

"Why are you out in the cold, if I may ask?"

He escorted her up the steps to Lady

DuFrayne's door and plied the knocker with vigor. "I have been to see the bishop."

Felicity's eyebrows flew up. "Bishop Stanhope?"

"Yes. As it happens, he is the only bishop with whom I am acquainted." He looked down at her and grinned. "You are agog to know what my purpose was in seeing him."

Felicity bit her lip. "I refrained, however, from asking you," she said, with great dignity.

"You are a model of self-possession."

Murdock opened the door and ushered them in, taking Sir Gavin's hat and greatcoat and Miss Pennington's pelisse. As they climbed the stairs to Lady DuFrayne's morning room, Gavin said, "By the by, if this weather holds, Mr. Stanhope is thinking of putting together a skating party."

"At his new house?"

"Yes. He says he has the perfect pond—large and shallow, and apparently frozen through by now. Is there somewhere in Bath where I could procure a pair of skates?"

Felicity was happy to recommend a shop, but as it turned out, the dry weather did not hold. The very next day it began to snow heavily, and the snow continued until the following Monday—the day when Mr. Stanhope had intended to host his skating party. Happily, his new property also encompassed a sloping, treeless hill, as perfect for sledding as his pond would have been for skating. So a quickly-penned flurry of notes was sent round to inform the invitees that the nature of the proposed entertainment had shifted, but the party would go forward as planned.

The snow lifted by mid-morning, although the sky remained cloudy. The Pennington sisters were allowed to borrow Aunt Agnes's carriage—since sledding was not her notion of entertainment—and Mrs. Pennington accompanied all four of her daughters to Mr. Stanhope's house. Everyone was curious to see it, and the snow on the road impeded their progress just enough to slow the carriage and give them a very good look at it as they approached.

Built of the local sandy-gold stone, it was a handsome, modern building set well back from the road behind a flat expanse that would doubtless prove to be a lawn once the winter passed. The aspect was pleasing and the setting was particularly pretty, with gentle hills sloping up behind the main house and woods marching along the top of the hills. It was difficult to determine how much land was attached to the house, since it was past the outskirts of town in an open area of farms and pastures. Although it was by no means grand it was clearly a gentleman's residence, and boasted two full storeys above the ground floor and a modest white portico at the main entrance. Its original owner, having built it in his westernmost field, had christened it simply "Westfield House."

Felicity saw Lulu's expression grow wistful as she gazed at Mr. Stanhope's home. She nudged her with her elbow and whispered to her. "Remember what we discussed, Lulu. Do not wear your heart on your sleeve."

Lulu blushed. "I said nothing!"

"No, but you were thinking very loudly."

The snow had been cleared from the drive, so once they had passed the gate they reached the entrance in less than a minute and were soon in Westfield's entry hall, which was crowded with laughing, chattering young people. Mr. Stanhope himself pushed through the throng and greeted them with every appearance of delight. It was clear that the party would be boisterous and informal. After the forced inactivity that the snowstorm had inflicted, everyone seemed eager to enjoy themselves out-of-doors.

Felicity was amused to see that Mr. Stanhope had even invited a few families with children—thus including a coterie of excited boys and girls whose noisy enthusiasm would act as a cover for the young adults. She admired his forethought. With so much exuberance surrounding them, decorum could be tossed to the wind; anyone might laugh and shout without drawing censure.

She spotted both of Mr. Stanhope's brothers among the crowd, speaking with Almeria Bliss and another lady she did not know. Nora and Helena darted off to join their particular friends, the Lawton girls. Gavin was here, too; easy to see across the room due to his height. But what caught her eye was the man standing quietly by the wall near Gavin. His plain clothing and unobtrusive demeanor marked him as a servant, but his remarkable appearance irresistibly drew her sympathetic interest. This must be the man Gavin had told her about—the manservant who had accompanied him from Bardados. His features were strong and striking, and his skin was nearly as dark as coffee. There could not be another such man in Bath. She wondered why Gavin had brought him to Mr. Stanhope's sledding party.

Gavin caught her eye then and nodded to her, beckoning her forward. She worked her way through the tumult until he was able to catch her elbow and draw her aside. "What a crush!" he said. "I would have come to you, Cousin, but I was afraid I'd never reach you, swimming against the tide."

"No indeed, most perilous," she retorted. "It was wise of you to leave it to me."

He laughed. "I caught you staring at Mr.

Ashanti and thought I would make him known to you."

"Was I staring?" She turned to include Mr. Ashanti in their conversation. "I beg your pardon. Sir Gavin has spoken warmly of you, and when I saw you I hoped I would have the chance to welcome you to England."

He looked surprised but gratified, and bowed very correctly. "T'ank you Miss," he said.

"This is Miss Pennington," said Gavin. "I see there is no need to introduce Mr. Ashanti."

"None at all," said Felicity cheerfully. "I daresay you will soon grow accustomed to being stared at, unfortunately. Pray do not regard it. You are destined to become a celebrity; not everyone is blessed with a personal history of such universal interest. Once it is known, the town will be abuzz. I feel I should congratulate you, but is that presumptuous? At any rate, I hope you will accept my best wishes for your future happiness and security." As Mr. Ashanti looked a little overwhelmed by all this, she turned to Gavin. "Will Mr. Ashanti be helping us sled?"

"Mr. Stanhope asked for all hands on deck, as it were, and I thought Mr. Ashanti might enjoy seeing a pleasanter aspect of winter. In town, it has been all discomfort and gloom—for those of us accustomed to sunny climes."

"You count yourself among the islanders, I perceive, despite your professed aversion to the place. Is a lifelong residence in England so easily forgotten?"

He grinned. "On the contrary. When the mercury dipped below forty, it all came back to me."

Westfield's central hall had two doorways on the left, leading to a parlor and a dining room, and two on the right, both opening onto a library that ran the length of the house on that side. Mr.

Stanhope had arranged for tea and conversation in the library, which is where Mama went to join the other, more sober, adults. Helena spied a pianoforte in the library as well, and headed for it like a bee to a flower. The rest of the party trooped through a vestibule at the end of the hall which led to a back door, and started across a field for the top of the hill.

"Keep left! Keep left!" shouted Mr. Stanhope, waving his arms good-humoredly at the bottom of the hill to prevent his guests from trampling the sledding ground. Children raced ahead on the appointed path. Lulu bounded up the hill among the children, whooping and laughing, and assisting some of the smaller ones who were struggling in the snow.

It did not seem a steep hill from the bottom, but from the top, Felicity thought, it looked to be a long way down. Several ladies were hanging back, exclaiming over it and declaring they would not dare to try the slope alone. This, naturally, spurred the men to gallantry. Mr. Stanhope had arranged to have all manner of sledding and sliding effects stacked at the top to await them—everything from actual sleds and toboggans to a couple of dented old tea trays that children might employ to slide about. All around her, young men were approaching the girls and offering to share a sled, in much the same way one solicits a lady's hand for a dance—and the girls were accepting with alacrity, although it was immediately apparent that sharing a sled with a gentleman would be even more daring than a waltz. A few blushed and bridled and weren't sure they should... but all were easily won over, once it was clear that no condemnation would follow. Everyone's parents, after all, had been left behind in Mr. Stanhope's library.

Felicity felt a touch on her elbow and

turned, surprised, to find Rev. Stanhope standing beside her. He bowed, looking a trifle self-conscious, and said, "Miss Pennington, I would be happy to escort you down the hill if you feel unequal to sledding alone."

She laughed. "Thank you, sir, but I am not at all afraid of sledding. I used to enjoy it very much—although it has been some years since I tried it."

He bowed again, and silently moved to the next lady. Felicity heard a low chuckle and turned to discover Gavin lurking nearby. "My dear Felicity, you have disappointed the good Reverend. You were supposed to feign maidenly qualms."

"Why?"

One dark eyebrow climbed higher on his forehead. "Why? Look around you." He waved a hand to indicate the couples lining up to share sleds. "I daresay half these shrinking violets are no more afraid of sledding than you are. They are merely seizing opportunity. It isn't every day a lady is offered a chance to embrace a gentleman in broad daylight. Where is your spirit of adventure?"

"Adventure. Is that what it would be?" She made a moue of distaste. "I suppose it is coldhearted of me, but the idea of embracing Rev. Stanhope—even for the few seconds necessary to sled down this hill—does not tempt me in the least."

He laughed out loud. "You are too fastidious."

At that moment, a boy about ten years old went flying down the hill on one of the tea trays, grabbing at the handles for dear life and hooting merrily. The metal disc careened madly across the slope and spun him around more than once, but he reached the bottom and managed, by flinging one leg out before him as a brake, to bump to a halt uninjured. He leapt to his feet and waved vigorously as his friends cheered.

"You see?" cried Mr. Stanhope, rubbing his hands together. "Even a child can do it!"

"Only a child can do it," called one of the men in the crowd.

Amid the laughter and good-natured chaffing that followed, Mr. Stanhope looked around him and, spotting Miss Bliss, held out his hand to her with a warm smile. "Come, Almeria! Let us show them how it's done."

Felicity was standing close enough to Miss Bliss to perceive the genuine fear in her eyes, and pitied her. Gavin was doubtless correct that many of the young ladies were pretending to feel more nervous than they truly did; Almeria was, she thought, attempting rather to hide the depth of her anxiety. Did Mr. Stanhope know her so little? It was almost cruel to turn everyone's attention to her, forcing her to choose between exposing her cowardice or risking her neck—as Almeria seemed to believe.

Thus appealed to, she smiled nervously. "I ought to have remained behind," she cried gaily. "I might even now be sipping hot tea before a fire."

Mr. Stanhope laughed. "And you shall," he promised. "But first, help me demonstrate to our friends how much fun is in store for them."

The poor girl had no choice but to come to him. He sat on a toboggan and seized the ropes. Laughing friends helped Almeria to sit between his legs. She looked petrified.

Felicity heard her say, "Oh, Oliver, are you quite sure this is safe?" before the toboggan abruptly slid over the crest and plunged down the hill. Almeria screamed.

It was over so quickly that no one had time

to discern whether her scream was one of terror, delight, or some mixture of the two. Felicity felt certain that it was a scream of unmixed terror. Almeria's body went absolutely rigid, which made steering difficult. Oliver ended up oversteering to the left and sent them flying into a snowbank. Almeria pitched helplessly, blindly forward into the snow—exactly as if she had squeezed her eyes shut, which Felicity felt certain she had—and floundered there, gasping and choking, until Mr. Stanhope pulled her out. He was laughing, but his laughter turned to concern as he belatedly realized that Miss Bliss was weeping from mingled fright, rage, and humiliation. She grabbed at his coat sleeves as he hauled her upright, but then struck him on the shoulder with her fist, panting some remark inaudible to the crowd at the top of the hill.

All around Felicity people were laughing and calling out encouragement. She feared that no one had taken Almeria Bliss's nerves seriously—and it was apparent that nobody had been hurt, so if Miss Bliss returned to the top of the hill she would likely receive little sympathy. However, she showed no inclination to climb the hill again. Mr. Ashanti and another manservant darted out from where they were stationed at the bottom of the hill, armed with whisks. They quickly brushed the snow from the couple's clothing, and Felicity watched as Almeria stalked off toward the house, alone. Mr. Stanhope looked sorry to see her go, but his duty was to his guests, after all, and he clearly could not abandon everyone else to accompany her. He hesitated for a moment, watching her, then knocked the snow from his toboggan, hoisted it onto his back, and, grinning, started up the path to the top once more.

Lulu, meanwhile, had been dashing

through the trees with several of the older children in an impromptu game of tag. She emerged now, laughing and breathless, with a ruddy-cheeked little girl in tow. One or two couples were selecting sleds from the jumble of possibilities, but they were being too slow about it for Felicity's intrepid sister. She seized a sled at random and dragged it to the edge of the lip. Seeing Mr. Stanhope climbing the hill below, she waved at him. "I'm taking Annie down!" she called, indicating the child. He waved back, then paused to watch as Lulu climbed onto the sled, settled the excited little girl before her, placed one arm protectively round her, and pushed off.

Annie's screams were definitely screams of laughter. Lulu took them neatly down the center of the run and skated them sideways at the bottom to slow their speed. The two men waiting at the bottom of the hill caught them and helped them off. Cheers erupted from the top of the hill, Mr. Stanhope grinned and clapped, and Annie danced frenziedly about, begging to do it again. Lulu rose, laughing, and bowed to her audience. Then Mr. Ashanti started up the hill before them, carrying the sled, while Lulu took little Annie's hand to help her navigate the path.

By the time they reached the top, the sledding party was truly underway. Boys on tea trays, children sharing sleds with adults, young men clasping young ladies, everyone was hurtling down the hill and climbing back up, and everyone was noisy and happy.

Mr. Ashanti returned the sled to the stack and turned to walk back down the path, but Gavin stopped him. "Not so fast, my friend. I didn't bring you here just to work."

And people laughed and cheered as the man who had never before seen snow sledded for the first time.

Felicity, secretly a bit stung by Gavin's characterization of her as overly fastidious, unbent sufficiently to share a toboggan after all—first with one of Nora's favorite young men, Mr. Lawton, and next with Rev. Stanhope. She noted with amusement that Gavin was making inroads with all the prettiest girls—as usual—flying down the hill first with Charlotte Lawton, then with Agnes Dickson, then with Jane Steele, then Miss Lawton again. She approached him between sledding engagements and rolled her eyes at him.

"What do you mean?" he demanded, brushing snow off his coat sleeve. "Faugh! I'm getting wet."

"Nothing in the world," she assured him. "I only wanted to caution you, you know, not to raise expectations by sledding more than twice with anyone."

"Are expectations so easily raised in Bath?"

"Oh, yes! There is generally little to do here, so feverish gossip is employed to relieve the tedium. You have already done more than enough to feature widely in tomorrow's conversations."

He looked skeptical. "What have I done?"

"One: You provided our small social circle with a new face." She ticked the points off on her gloved fingers. "Two: You are single—which, of itself, is sufficient to arouse interest in many quarters. Three: You have had the temerity to arrive in town with a baronetcy already firmly in your grasp. Four—"

But Gavin interrupted her, pointing past her shoulder. "You won't want to miss this. Look at Lulu."

She turned and saw Lulu, blushing adorably, climbing onto a sled with Mr. Stanhope. While Stanhope busied himself tugging at his gloves, bracing his feet and gathering the ropes, Lulu leaned blissfully back against his chest, looking as if she hoped never to leave Mr. Stanhope's arms again.

"Oh, *Lulu*," murmured Felicity, distressed. She bit her lip. Had anyone else noticed how besotted Lulu was? Her eyes darted anxiously around the circle surrounding the sled, but it was entirely comprised of men, and their attention seemed to be on the sled itself. But why had the sled been dragged so far back from the edge of the hill?

The answer came at once. Two men bent to seize the back of the sled. They ran toward the hill's edge, pushing it ahead of them with all their might. A little scream of fright escaped Felicity, but too late; the men shoved the sled over the lip and it went flying—quite literally flying—into the air for a moment before dropping, hard, onto the slope. The push sent it off at a dizzying rate of speed.

As one, Lulu and Mr. Stanhope leaned this way and that, sending the sled ripping to the right, then to the left, snow spraying from the runners. The sled was moving too fast for the ride to last long, or Felicity feared her heart might stop as she watched. "Ware the bottom!" she cried, knowing they could not hear her—by this time, all the sledding had scraped the flat at the bottom of the hill nearly clear of snow, and the bare ground would have been dangerous indeed to hit at such a high rate of speed. But evidently Mr. Stanhope had thought of that. Together, he and Lulu leaned to their right at just the correct moment, the sled headed left—hit a rock— whooshed into the air again—and then plowed deeply into the same snowbank that Mr. Stanhope and Almeria had ended up in earlier. This time, obviously, the landing was deliberate, head-first, and far deeper. The front half of the sled completely disappeared into the snow.

Felicity clapped her hands to her cheeks, her eyes nearly starting from her head. But Lulu and Mr. Stanhope crawled uninjured from the snowbank, whooping with laughter, so crusted with white that they looked like two polar bears emerging from their den. Mr. Stanhope reached his hand to Lulu and pulled her, stumbling and gasping, out of the thickest part of the drift and into his arms, where he promptly whirled her round in an exuberant circle. By this time, Mr. Ashanti and the other manservant had reached them, whisks in hand, and all was laughter and confusion as they submitted to having the snow vigorously brushed from their clothing.

Felicity felt she could breathe again. Beside her, Gavin stuck two fingers in his mouth and whistled like a boy, causing Mr. Stanhope to look up the hill. He then cupped his hands around his mouth and shouted, "Well done!"

As Mr. Stanhope and Lulu laughed and bowed, Felicity gave Gavin an indignant little shove. "Well done? It was dangerous!"

Gavin grinned. "Yes, but you must own it was very well done! I never knew Lulu had so much pluck. Let's help get the sledding gear to the bottom of the hill, shall we? I believe we're all going back to the house."

Getting the gear to the bottom of the hill simply meant that those who remained at the top of the hill climbed on sleds and sledded down. Gavin seized one of the last remaining sleds, dragged it to the lip of the hill, and beckoned to Felicity. She approached, but eyed it dubiously.

"Gavin, this one is too small for both of us."

"Nonsense. Sit forward, place your feet on the brace here, and tuck your skirts beneath you."

"And where will you sit?" asked Felicity,

following his sanguine instructions. "I am taking up the entire sled."

"I'll manage," he said cheerfully. "Give me another inch, Cousin."

"I am not your cousin, and I am already nearly hugging my knees," she complained, laughing.

"Then hug them," he retorted, and settled himself behind her.

Gavin's long legs stretched easily past her and his booted feet braced beside hers on the sled runners. His thighs pressed warmly against her sides; she could actually feel the muscles bunch as his legs hugged her body. His arms encircled her too, as he grasped the ropes. Felicity found herself snugly embraced by Gavin's long, lean body and blushed. Unsettling, unfamiliar emotions raced through her. Why, she wondered confusedly, had she felt nothing of the kind when sledding with Rev. Stanhope or Mr. Lawton? She very much feared that she now understood Lulu's reaction to Mr. Stanhope. She hoped to high heaven that she was less transparent. But there was no need, in her situation, to lean back into Gavin's embrace—it was inescapable; they were pressed together willy-nilly by the smallness of the sled.

And she liked it. She liked it very much indeed.

Oh dear.

There wasn't time to think, let alone grow accustomed to the novelty. Gavin pushed off and they flew down the hill, his chest pressed against her back, his limbs securely gripping her as the cold air rushed past her face. She laughed from pure joy; she couldn't help it. And then it was over. The sled bumped to a halt, hands reached down to pull her to her feet, and with a shake and a whisk she returned to normalcy—hoping that the chill would account for the pinkness of her cheeks.

## Chapter Nine

The warmth of the house smote their cold faces with welcome relief from the winter air as Oliver shepherded his noisy, happy party back into the hall. Everyone divested themselves of their wet outergarments, discarding them, at his instruction, onto the marble-topped tables that lined the walls, where his staff stood ready to remove them for drying and pressing. He then ushered everyone into his library, remarking, "I thought this was a large room until this moment! Allow me, Miss Steele—if you will step this way, Mr. Beaufort—Annie, I think your mama has room for you—" And he busied himself for a minute or two finding places for everyone to sit, which became possible only when most of the young boys willingly sat on the floor.

It was exactly the kind of party he liked best: crowded, cozy, cheerful and informal. A hum of conversation swelled. The boys played jack-stones on his hearth rug. Several people gathered by the pianoforte and sang Christmas carols to Miss Helena Pennington's accompaniment. A wood fire crackled on the hearth. Little Annie fell asleep on her mother's lap. It was very like a family party, he thought happily—the sort of family party he had rarely experienced in his own family circle, which was small and usually a little too quiet for his taste. Now that he had his own home, he could fill it with congenial souls as often as he liked. The contemplation of this glad prospect made his eyes sparkle with anticipatory delight.

A word to his newly-hired housekeeper, and refreshments were served: tea and hot cider, sherry and mulled wine, biscuits, cheese— everything passed round on little plates so that his guests need not crowd round a table. He was pleased. It was all just as he had hoped it would be, and his friends were visibly enjoying themselves. Even his shy brother Charles had found people to talk to, and was playing backgammon in a corner of the room.

His eyes finally lit on Almeria, who was sitting beside her mother and appearing more than usually subdued. With a pang, he recalled that he owed her an apology. He set down his teacup and went to her.

After greeting Mrs. Bliss he bowed over Almeria's hand, patting it gently. "I am glad to see you have recovered from our little spill. You left so quickly that I had no chance to beg your pardon." He turned, smiling, to include her mother in the conversation. "Did Almeria tell you? We were the first down the hill, but landed unluckily in a snowbank. My fault, I fear."

Mrs. Bliss returned his smile, but faintly. "Yes," she replied. "It is a miracle you both escaped uninjured. Really, Oliver, I would not have entrusted my daughter to your care, had I believed you capable of such poor judgment."

His smile faded. Almeria pulled her hand from his and folded her hands in her lap. Her gaze was fixed steadily on a point just over his left shoulder. Was she too angry to look him in the eye? He studied Almeria's set expression, then looked back at the reproof in Mrs. Bliss's eyes.

"Poor judgment," he repeated, stunned. He tried to laugh. "But it was nothing at all. The sort of mishap that commonly happens in the course of a morning spent sledding."

"No doubt," said Almeria tightly. "Which is why sledding is a children's pastime, Oliver, unsuitable for adults."

His mind flooded with the vivid picture of Lulu Pennington, laughing and rosy, enthusiastically sledding down that hill—first with every child who asked for her help, and lastly with him—game as a pebble and loving every minute of it. He longed to tell Almeria how poorly her behavior contrasted with Miss Lulu's— but that would be petty. Useless, too, since she would interpret Miss Pennington's enjoyment of the day as further evidence of her immaturity and lack of discipline.

"I am sorry that you did not enjoy my party, Almeria," he said quietly, and bowed. She looked at him then, and he saw remorse and dismay in her expression—she opened her lips to speak, either to apologize or explain; he knew not which, and, at the moment, did not care. He walked away, so disturbed by the encounter that he actually felt grateful that he had not, as yet, proposed marriage to her. He would need to think on the matter—a matter that he had believed, an hour ago, was a settled certainty, awaiting only the right moment. It was disquieting to find that one could harbor doubts about such an important thing. Once a man made up his mind, begad, he wanted to act. Not dither.

After his guests departed, he ate a simple dinner in solitary state in his new dining room. The house was not yet completely furnished, but the main rooms were coming along nicely, and he was pleased with his staff—particularly the

Tiptons, the middle-aged couple who served as housekeeper and butler. At the moment, his household consisted of a cook, the Tiptons, the cook's son—a boy who served as bootblack, clock-winder, silver-polisher, and Oliver wasn't sure what-all—and a housemaid. Five servants! And a groom for his horses, which made six. Good heavens, there were half a dozen people dependent on him, and he had yet to take a wife. He grinned, amused at the thought of Oliver Stanhope, lord of the manor.

But there was no one present to share the joke.

His amusement faded and he frowned into his wine, thinking. Almeria. He had been picturing Almeria at the other end of this table. Almeria directing the housekeeper. Almeria sharing his home, adding little feminine touches, doing whatever mysterious things women did all day. He was fairly certain she expected his proposal. It certainly seemed that both families expected it. The Stanhopes and the Blisses had been friends since before he was born. He had known Almeria all his life. Her character was above reproach, her family and background a perfect fit, and she was generally held to be a pretty girl, although...

Although he had never found her particularly attractive.

Oliver pushed back from the table, irritated. He disliked entertaining doubts. There was nothing wrong with Almeria. He had recently become aware of a few little quirks in her, that's all. Nobody was perfect.

And yet, as he climbed the stairs to his bed chamber, the thought niggled at him that perhaps Almeria would be perfect for...or at least compatible with...a different man. Not him.

And for the first time, it occurred to him

that she might refuse his offer. What a facer that would be! Was that possible? Might she, too, be wondering if he were the right choice? Oliver Stanhope, with his fast horses and love of informality, might make a straitlaced, nervous woman unhappy.

As unhappy as she might make him.

Really, he had to give this more thought.

Chapter Ten

Meanwhile, in Henrietta Street, Felicity Pennington could not sleep. Beside her, Nora lay curled like a kitten, murmuring as she dreamed. Felicity lay flat on her back and stared at the ceiling, unable to still her whirling thoughts. She was rarely troubled by insomnia. Perhaps it was the moonlight stealing in through the curtain chinks. Perhaps it was the hall clock striking in the stillness. Perhaps she had drunk too much tea.

She knew it was none of these things.

"Botheration," she muttered crossly. It was Gavin DuFrayne who was keeping her awake. She rolled onto her side and punched her pillow, hoping that if she got comfortable enough she would fall asleep despite the clamor in her brain.

Felicity harbored no illusions about herself. She thought it best to know what one was, accept it, and make the best of it. Men liked her very well, but they did not fall in love with her. Gavin DuFrayne, on the other hand, had been casting girls' hearts into a flutter since he was fourteen. She had no more hope of catching his eye than the freckled milkmaid who delivered Aunt Agnes's butter and cheese. She must not indulge foolish thoughts about a man she could

116

not have. Not only would she make herself ridiculous, she might make herself deeply unhappy as well.

Besides which (she told herself firmly) any absurdity on her part might ruin their barely-rekindled friendship, and she would hate to have that happen. And besides *that* (she reminded herself), she and Gavin were, if anything, adversaries. Or at least rivals. They were in competition with each other for Aunt Agnes's regard, were they not? At least Gavin seemed to think so. She must tread carefully when dealing with any member of a family that harbored so much ill-will toward her own. If Gavin could cut her out of their aunt's good graces, he would do it in a heartbeat, she had no doubt.

She did sleep, eventually, but vivid dreams filled her head and she was glad to wake and return to reality. As she dressed her hair she pulled a face at her reflection in the flecked and murky mirror of the vanity she shared with Nora. "No more," she told the face in the glass.

Nora's face popped around the corner of the door. "No more what?"

Felicity threw a comb at her. "No more snooping, Eleanora Nosy."

She had promised to accompany Aunt Agnes to the Pump Room today, and was annoyed, but not surprised, when Gavin attached himself to the expedition. When they gathered in the hall, preparing to go, she tried giving him a severe look behind Aunt Agnes's back. He then pasted such an absurdly innocent expression on his face that she laughed aloud.

"The Pump Room," said Gavin plaintively, "is one of Bath's most famous landmarks, and I have never seen it."

"Poor thing," said Felicity sympathetically.

Aunt Agnes looked sharply from Gavin to

Felicity and back again. "Well? We are about to remedy that. Are you two chaffing each other?"

"Yes, ma'am."

"Well, stop it. Gavin, give me your arm. My cane, Murdock. Felicity, you must needs walk behind us with Henry; there will not be room on the pavement for the three of us to walk together."

Felicity had foreseen this. It was one of the reasons she was cross that Gavin had invited himself along. The other reason was that Gavin, like a well-trained sheepdog, kept separating her from her aunt—and Aunt Agnes frequently, albeit unwittingly, aided his maneuvers. Today, for instance. Normally Lady DuFrayne's footman, Henry, trailed behind them as they walked to the Pump Room; today Felicity would be walking beside Henry in silence as Aunt Agnes leaned on Gavin's arm and chatted with her nephew.

Still, even accounting for the minor hazards inflicted by winter on the pavement, the walk was a short one. Ten minutes of fresh, cold air and they were there. The DuFrayne party entered the Pump Room, Sir Gavin DuFrayne's name was entered in the subscription book, Aunt Agnes handed her cane to Henry, and they were free to stroll about the room three abreast if they chose.

Gavin surveyed the room with an interested air. "A handsome room filled with handsome people," he said. "This is delightful."

"The musicians are excellent," said Felicity. She pointed at the entrance to the music gallery. "Helena comes as often as she can and sits right there, refusing to speak to anyone for half an hour at a time."

Gavin turned to their aunt. "Do you take the waters, ma'am? Shall I fetch a cup for you?"

"Certainly not. They are vile. Let us take a

turn about the room so I can introduce you to Mrs. Carroll; I see her over by the window there. Then you may find a place for me by the fire."

The execution of this plan took a considerable amount of time. Lady DuFrayne's acquaintance was wide, and her consequence great. As she progressed slowly round the colonnaded perimeter of the Pump Room, party after party hailed her, bowing and requesting introduction to her nephew. At the end of this royal procession, Lady DuFrayne was ushered to the seat she had requested by one of the two fires—procured for her, and guarded by, Henry. There she sat, resplendent in blue lustring, her footman standing behind her chair, her cane restored to her so she might rest her outstretched hand upon it, looking for all the world like a medieval queen receiving supplicants as the good citizens of Bath approached her, one by one and two by two.

Felicity stood a little apart, watching with amusement. This was just the sort of morning Aunt Agnes loved, and having Gavin to show off was a novelty the likes of which she had not enjoyed for years. Poor Gavin found himself thrust to the center of Aunt Agnes's stage, displayed like a two-headed pig at the fair. He handled it gracefully, but Felicity frequently had to cover her mouth to hide her smile as she watched. She thought, quite frankly, that it served him right.

Eventually he escaped Aunt Agnes's orbit and came to her—his expression like a hunted creature. She laughed aloud. "Shall I fetch you a glass of the waters, Gavin? You look decidedly unwell."

He took out his handkerchief and dabbed at his brow. "Just a trifle warm," he said. "Having stood so close to the fire. Phew!"

"You *would* come," she pointed out. "I tried to give you a hint."

"Am I expected to remember all these people?"

"It won't matter. They will remember you." He looked so dismayed that another gurgle of laughter escaped her. "You entered your name in the book, so an announcement of your presence in Bath will be published in the newspaper. You will be showered with invitations."

"Good God!"

"Indeed."

"But half the people here are invalids. Did you see those poor chaps with the gout? And the dowager with the enormous goiter? They won't be dancing anytime soon."

"There are other ways to pass a winter's evening. After all, everyone must eat dinner."

Gavin dabbed at his forehead again. "Perhaps I'll try the waters after all."

This time she pealed so merrily that several people turned to look at her. Embarrassed, she tried to turn her laughter into a cough.

"Unconvincing," Gavin told her. "But here come the Stanhopes. That Friday-faced vicar ought to sober you up."

"He is not Friday-faced," she said indignantly. "He merely has a serious approach to life."

But the Stanhopes were nearly on them now, so she turned her attention to them. Oliver Stanhope was not among the party; it was the bishop, his wife, and the two sons who were staying with them for Christmas. After exchanging bows and pleasantries, Felicity was ready to move on, but could not. Gavin had pulled the bishop aside and left her with Mrs. Stanhope, James and Charles. And then, as luck would have it, Mrs. Stanhope went off on Charles's arm to greet another acquaintance, leaving her alone with Rev. Stanhope.

He gave her a rather strained smile. "Did you enjoy the sledding yesterday, Miss Pennington?"

"I did," she replied. "Although I own I am feeling it a bit today! It has been years since I sledded."

"The same is true for me. And doubtless for most, if not all, who attended! Save for the children, of course. A novel idea for a party, I thought. I'm afraid Oliver rarely considers propriety when there is merriment to be had."

His smile was definitely strained. He seemed to be worried that she might have been offended by his brother's idea of fun—or his own participation in it—and was watching her expression apprehensively, as if he expected her to disapprove. She was surprised by this, but his next remark helped her to understand his disquiet: "In my religious capacity, perhaps I ought to have said something. Pointed my brother in a different direction, you know. My father saw nothing amiss with the scheme, and I do not like to set my own judgment up against his—as I'm sure you can understand—but it's possible my father did not foresee the excesses such an activity would encourage. I know I did not."

"Excesses?" Felicity stared blankly at him. When his discomfort visibly increased she understood at last. "Oh! All the noise and confusion, I suppose you mean. Couples sharing a sled. Young ladies escaping from their chaperones. Was it so shocking?" She smiled. "Pray do not bludgeon your conscience over a trifle, Rev. Stanhope. It was all in good fun, and among friends and family. In the open air, too! Forgive me, but it would be very odd of you to find fault with it now. If recollection serves, you shared a sled yourself."

"Only with the most respectable of women," he said earnestly. "I would not have you think that I chose lightly."

"Certainly not," she said, but her reply was automatic. What on earth was the good vicar's meaning? Was he trying to compliment her? She glanced at Gavin, hoping he would come and rescue her, but he was deep in conversation with the bishop. They seemed to be talking very earnestly together, and she could not catch his eye without Rev. Stanhope perceiving her signal.

"Do you skate, Miss Pennington?"

"Yes, but not well." She wrinkled her nose. "I manage to stay upright, for the most part, but I wouldn't win any races. Is your brother revisiting the idea of a skating party?"

"If the weather holds, I believe he—" But before he could finish his answer, his mother and brother Charles rejoined them, Mrs. Stanhope requesting that he come and greet Lady DuFrayne, who was preparing to leave.

Felicity went with them and was finally able to catch Gavin's eye. He was still speaking to the bishop but brought the conversation to an end when he perceived that his aunt was standing. Gavin and Bishop Stanhope joined them briefly, then the Stanhopes parted company with Felicity and the DuFraynes, who exited the Pump Room.

"A very pleasant hour," said Lady DuFrayne, with great satisfaction as Felicity and Henry helped her arrange her shawls. "Most refreshing. What did you think of our Pump Room, Gavin?"

"Beautiful, ma'am."

"And the company to be found in Bath?"

"Genteel, to be sure, and agreeable as

well."

She poked him with her cane. "Better than Barbados, I'll warrant. Ha! Walk with Henry, Gavin, I've something to say to Felicity."

Felicity suppressed an urge to stick her tongue out at Gavin. She held Aunt Agnes's arm and they began the stroll back to Laura Place with Henry and Gavin behind them. "I hope what you have to say is not confidential, Aunt, because I know for a fact that Gavin is not above eavesdropping."

"I heard that," said Gavin.

Lady DuFrayne chuckled. "Lower your voice, Felicity. And tell me what you think of James Stanhope. I saw you speaking with him."

"Good heavens, Aunt Agnes, how did you find time to notice such a thing while holding court with so many people?"

Lady DuFrayne's eyes gleamed up at her. "I was looking for it, missy. There, now! I've no wish to meddle, but I take an interest in these matters."

Felicity bit her lip. "You've every right to take an interest," she admitted. "And, to be perfectly fair, you've every right to meddle. You've been sponsoring me for years."

"Pish-tosh," retorted Aunt Agnes. "I do as I please."

"And would it please you if I took an interest in Rev. Stanhope?"

"Of course it would, child." She snorted. "Frankly, Felicity, it would please me if you showed interest in anyone at all. But a son of the Stanhopes? I own, I would be delighted to see you so respectably settled. And naturally it would add to my pleasure if you attached yourself to the son of my very good friends."

"Naturally." Felicity sighed—then caught herself, ashamed. This was no way to repay Aunt

Agnes for all her kindness. "Rev. Stanhope is very..." She searched for a word that might praise the good vicar without unduly raising Aunt Agnes's hopes. "Worthy," she finished.

"Hm!" Aunt Agnes's lips twitched. "Thank you, Felicity, I now know exactly what you think of him. I was young myself once. I never felt the slightest interest in *worthy* gentlemen, and I daresay you don't either."

Felicity, feeling guilty, patted her aunt's arm. "I'm sorry, Aunt Agnes. Perhaps Rev. Stanhope has a few redeeming faults. I will try to find them."

## Chapter Eleven

Lulu and Helena slipped into a pew near the back of the nave. Helena loved to come and listen to the organist practice, and today Lulu had accompanied her, thinking it might calm her restless spirit. But as the ethereal music swelled all around her and the winter sunlight poured through the high, arched windows, the beauty and peace of the abbey only served to intensify her emotions. She closed her eyes and gave herself up to the longing that filled her soul these days.

Would it be wrong to pray for Oliver Stanhope to notice her? She supposed it would. God doubtless had more important matters to attend to.

But just as if the Almighty heard the unspoken wish of her heart, as she and Helena exited the cathedral she very nearly collided with Mr. Stanhope himself. She was so startled that she almost tripped on the step. He steadied her briefly with his hand, laughing.

"Miss Pennington!" he exclaimed, looking delighted. "And it's Miss Helena, is it not? Yes, I thought I recognized you. How do you do?"

Lulu stammered something incoherent, but he seemed not to notice her confusion. They

exchanged bows and pleasantries, and Helena—
momentarily lifted from her shyness by the
lingering thrall of music—satisfied his curiosity
as to what brought them to the abbey on a mid-
week morning. "I often come to hear Mr. Field
play," she confessed, glowing. "How I wish I were
a real musician!"

"You are a very fine musician," said Lulu
indignantly.

But Helena shook her head. "Not really,"
she said. "Not like that."

"You play the pianoforte beautifully," said
Mr. Stanhope. "I very much enjoyed hearing you
the other day."

Helena hung her head, blushing hotly,
mumbled some disclaimer, and returned to her
usual tongue-tied silence. By this time, however,
Lulu had recovered her composure and was able
to speak normally. "You shouldn't compliment
her," she explained to Mr. Stanhope. "It lowers
her opinion of your taste."

Helena cried out at this, but Mr. Stanhope
laughed. "Very well. I shall refrain from giving my
opinion, although I spoke only the truth. For my
part, I enjoy singing but wish I could play an
instrument. There! I would never have the
patience to learn. I'm told one cannot excel
without practice, and as there is nothing more
painful to me than hearing badly-played music, I
would never practice."

Even Helena laughed at this, but it was
clear she was still uncomfortable. Lulu took pity
on her sister and shouldered the conversational
burden, allowing Helena to fade into the
background as she and Mr. Stanhope laughed
and talked with great animation. In fact, the
conversation was so agreeable that they lost track
of time. It was only when Helena touched Lulu's
sleeve and reminded her that Mama would

wonder what had become of them that she realized they had been standing in the square in front of the abbey for half an hour.

"I beg your pardon," exclaimed Mr. Stanhope, looking surprised. "I had not meant to detain you. My own business in town is complete, so I was on my way to the Pump Room—but it was unconscionable of me to behave as if you ladies are equally at leisure."

"But we are," said Lulu. "That is—I should speak for myself only. My sister likes to get back to her instrument while the organ music still rings in her ears."

Mr. Stanhope declared himself to be at the Pennington sisters' disposal and escorted them back to their very doorstep, although he declined an invitation to come inside. He seemed to hesitate on the stoop, and then wondered aloud if Miss Lulu had any interest in visiting the Pump Room—as the weather was so fine and dry today. "I would be most happy to escort you there and back again if you should desire it," he said.

Lulu's heart leapt while she pretended to hesitate. But while she paused, Mr. Stanhope's face turned a little red. "I suppose it is a silly idea," he said, half-laughing, "since we just came from there."

"Not at all," said Lulu quickly. "It was kind of you to walk Helena home. I would be happy to return with you, if you like. After all, it is only a step from here."

And so, inwardly rejoicing at Henrietta Street's lucky proximity to the Pump Room, Lulu took Mr. Stanhope's arm and lost herself once more in the pleasure of his company. When the Pump Room proved too crowded and noisy, they walked to the Crescent and strolled up and down, deep in conversation. What, exactly, they talked about she could not afterward recall. Certainly they each described their childhoods, but apart from that she could not say. It simply seemed that they held similar opinions on nearly everything, and on the points where they differed, the differences led to spirited, fascinated discussion rather than disagreement. They laughed at the same things. They enjoyed the same books. The day passed as if in a dream, and only the dipping sun recalled them to a sense of time and place. Mr. Stanhope hastened, then, to return Lulu to her home before sunset—but made her happy day complete by asking if he might take her out in his curricle on Thursday. Since Lulu did not share Miss Bliss's fear of fast horses, he was eager to show her the paces of his favorite gelding. Lulu assented to the scheme with barely-contained enthusiasm.

She then bade Mr. Stanhope a very correct, demure adieu. But once the front door was closed between them, she fairly danced through the house, hugging herself.

Felicity popped out of the bedchamber she shared with Nora just as Lulu was returning her pelisse to its customary peg outside the door of the smaller chamber she shared with Helena. "Where on earth have you been? Mama was ready to send for the constable."

Lulu laughed and pulled a face. "Nowhere at all!"

Felicity raised an eyebrow. "Helena said Mr. Stanhope spirited you away. Were you with him all this time? It's been hours."

"And very pleasant hours they were," retorted Lulu, pulling off her gloves. Humming, she returned to her room to stuff her discarded gloves in a drawer.

Felicity followed her, looking perturbed. "Lulu, really—it simply isn't done. A lady doesn't go off alone with a man she scarcely knows, for

128

hours on end—"

"He's a very respectable man, Felicity. For pity's sake—he's Bishop Stanhope's son! And I know perfectly well you've ridden in gentlemen's curricles without a chaperone, in London."

"Riding in a gentleman's curricle, in the open air, in a public place, is an entirely different matter."

"I am glad to hear it," said Lulu, favoring her sister with a saucy grin. "Because that is exactly the plan we made for Thursday."

Felicity sank onto the bed, seemingly unnerved. "Good heavens."

Lulu pulled the last pins out of her hat and tossed it happily into the air.

Felicity caught it. "Lulu pray, *pray* do not get your hopes up. I very much fear you will break your heart if Mr. Stanhope offers for Miss Bliss."

"Yes, but perhaps he will not offer for her." Lulu spun round in a happy circle.

"Oh, Lulu." Felicity caught her hands, stopping her mid-twirl. Lulu was surprised to see the distress in her sister's face. "Very few people marry to disoblige their families. If both their families expect them to marry, I think he will, in fact, offer for Almeria one day."

And up the hill, in his mother's parlor, Oliver Stanhope was at that moment receiving much the same message. He found his mother embroidering by lamplight, and as he bent to kiss her cheek in greeting, she commented on the lateness of the hour. "I expected you some time ago, Oliver. You had better stay for dinner. You will be riding home in full dark now, one way or the other."

"I would gladly stay, ma'am, but I told my staff to expect me."

"Your staff." Mrs. Stanhope smiled. "I

forget you are a gentleman of property now. How quickly you have established yourself! Are you pleased with the Tiptons?"

"Exceedingly pleased." Oliver set down his hat and sat across from his mother, regaling her with tales of the excellence of his cook, the masterful degree of cleanliness and comfort engineered by his housekeeper, and how generally delightful he found his new home to be.

"And do you order everything yourself, or leave the running of the house to Mrs. Tipton?"

He waved a hand. "Oh, well, I know nothing of such things. So far I have ceded the authority to her, and she seems to be expert at what she does. I've no complaints."

"Take care, Oliver. A single gentleman—especially one as easy-going as you—might easily be taken advantage of."

He opened his eyes at this. "Overspending, do you mean? Surely not."

Mrs. Stanhope set down her silks. "Dear me, I didn't mean to imply that the Tiptons are dishonest. But until you take a wife, you must look over the household accounts yourself."

A rather fraught pause ensued. It seemed to Oliver that his mother was watching him keenly—but having dropped the hint, she said nothing more. Mother was nothing if not discreet.

He gave her a rueful smile. "You are hoping I turn those duties over to a wife sooner rather than later."

"I own, it would gladden my heart to see you settled."

"I am settled, Mother."

"You are speaking of your house. I am speaking of something else. Something a little more important, even, than that."

"Yes! Marriage." He gave an uneasy little laugh. "Why is it, I wonder, that mothers are so anxious for their children to marry?"

"We want to see our children happy." She lifted an eyebrow at him. "When last we spoke on the subject—some time ago—you seemed to be looking forward to the prospect with pleasure."

Oliver shifted uncomfortably in his chair. He remembered that conversation. At the time, he had still been looking for a house. He had entertained vague, but rosy, visions of buying a place and installing Almeria as its mistress more-or-less simultaneously. In hindsight, perhaps he ought not to have confided those notions to his mother.

"I do intend to marry, Mother, and I hope it will be soon."

Her face lit with pleasure. "That is excellent news. Almeria will be so pleased! I think she had begun to doubt your intentions—just lately, you know. But I daresay you have found yourself busier than you anticipated, moving in to Westfield. There are always a thousand details—"

He was forced to interrupt her. "Hold, please, Mother—you have run well ahead of me. I am not on the point of offering for Almeria Bliss." The expression on his mother's face struck dread into his heart. "Egad! Is she expecting it?"

Her hands flew to her cheeks. "Oliver! She has been expecting it any time these past three years!"

He stared. "Three years! How is that possible? You must be mistaken. I have not entertained the thought for longer than the past six months!"

She rose and took a hasty turn about the room, wringing her hands. "Oh, this is calamity. We all assumed—Caroline and I certainly assumed—"

"Mother, whatever schemes you may have hatched with Almeria's mother—"

"It is not a *scheme.* You have known—you must have known—it is the dearest wish of our hearts! Surely we have spoken of it a hundred times. Since you were children, both families have desired it. Such an eligible match—so suitable in every way! So *obvious.* Oliver, you cannot pretend you did not know."

No, in fact, he couldn't. Honesty forced him to acknowledge that he had long known about this idea, and until lately had considered it a rather pleasant one. He wondered if he ought to disclose to her the faults he had lately glimpsed in Almeria—her taste for cruel gossip, her judgmentalism. No. It would be ungentlemanly. And hypocritical as well, since what he disliked most in Almeria's conduct was her repeating tales about others.

"The truth is, I have been going along with the notion—but merely entertaining it as a possibility. I never realized—I didn't know—although I feared—oh hang it all! It seems the rest of you are more serious about it than ever I was." He rose and crossed to her, taking her restless hands in his own and clasping them strongly. "You must tell me. Did you speak to Mrs. Bliss—or, worse, Almeria—on this subject after our conversation last spring? I was rambling. Thinking aloud. Surely you did not..." But his voice trailed off as he saw, by her expression, that she had. He groaned and dropped her hands. "You did."

"On such a subject, mothers do talk." Her color was heightened, but she did not look sorry. "And it is only natural for the mother of a daughter to share the contents of these conversations with her child. Almeria has been encouraged since the day she was old enough to think of such things, to view you as her future partner. I've no wish to impose the match on you if you are unwilling—"

"Well, thank God for that!"

"—but I see no reason why you should be unwilling."

"I am fond of Almeria. But I do not love her in the way I hope to love my wife."

She looked relieved. "Oh, if that is all—! Such feelings rightly arrive after the wedding, Oliver, not before it. Your father and I were matched by our parents, you know—a custom that was already falling out of favor, even then— but who better to choose a life partner for you, than those who know you best? I see no evidence that the prevailing mode of allowing young persons to choose for themselves has met with any greater success than the old-fashioned way. Your father and I have been perfectly content."

He shook his head, half laughing, half groaning. "Oh, Mother. You and Father are both so even-tempered you might have been content with anyone. Alas, I am not so malleable. I think I must find someone who matches me to begin with, not try to buckle myself—or my bride—into an ill-fitting harness."

She frowned. "You are romantic."

"Then I must find a romantic woman. That, at least, ought not to be difficult. Many young women today are romantic, I hear."

"Do not jest." Real anger flashed in her eyes. "What of duty, Oliver? What of honor? Do you feel no obligation to Almeria—a lady of unimpeachable character, well known to you, as is her family—a girl with whom you are closely acquainted and, as you yourself say, you already feel some degree of affection toward? Will you jilt her?"

"I cannot jilt her. I have not offered for her."

"But you *should.*"

He raked his hand distractedly through his hair again and began to pace. "I do not mean to criticize you, Mother, but you ought not to have encouraged her. I have by no means made up my mind."

She returned to her chair and sank into it, lips tightly compressed. "You are determined, then, to keep her dangling while you chase other women. I had thought better of you, Oliver."

Stated so baldly, it did sound bad. Was that what he was doing? A brief image of Lulu Pennington rose before his eyes, her laughing blue eyes turned up to his, and he felt a pang. "She needn't *dangle*. Almeria is free to follow her own heart."

She snipped a thread and stabbed a needle into her embroidery with, it seemed to Oliver, unnecessary force. Her lips were still tight with disapproval. "It is my understanding," she said in clipped tones, "that Almeria's interest is already fixed. On you."

Guilt and remorse shot through him. Oliver sat and tried to smile. "Then we must hope I come to my senses, I suppose. Although I warn you, I would not bank on it."

"No. And it grieves me to say, nor would I." Stab, stab. She was not looking at him.

"You probably wonder if will choose a bride as impulsively as I chose a house. Spit-spot, there she is, make an offer and the thing is done."

"It does seem to be your way, Oliver. And I take leave to point out, it is no way to choose a wife."

"Normally I would agree. But the day I saw it, I knew Westfield was precisely what I had been looking for." She glanced at him, frowning, and he quirked an eyebrow at her. "Perhaps the same thing will happen with a wife. I'll know when I have found the right woman for me. That can happen, I'm told."

She looked disturbed. "People are not houses, Oliver, and a wife cannot be easily discarded. It would be foolish to pin your hopes of happiness on an unknown girl."

"I was jesting again, a little," he admitted. "And I ought not."

"No," she said. "You ought not. And you know I often misunderstand your jests." She set down her silks and looked at him levelly. "What am I to say to Caroline?"

"Nothing," he said firmly. Her meddling had done enough. But he could not scold his mother. "I will speak to Almeria when the time is right."

"I hope you do," she said, almost inaudibly, and returned to her embroidery.

He rode home through the cold moonlight with his emotions in an unaccustomed tumult. He almost wished he hadn't invited Lulu to take a spin in his curricle. Was it wrong to enjoy her company so much, when he was all-but-promised to Almeria?

Then he remembered the way she laughed and discovered he couldn't regret it. He liked her, dash it all. And before he stepped into parson's mousetrap, he had better be certain he'd picked the right mouse.

## Chapter Twelve

Gavin was not a devotee of the Pump Room. However, as a guest of Lady DuFrayne, he found himself there more often than his own inclination would have prompted. The Pump Room formed the center of his aunt's social circle, so she visited it at least two or three times weekly. Each morning spent gossiping and parading up and down refreshed her as water restores a garden. She declared it was better than a newspaper for keeping her abreast of Bath's goings-on. Felicity normally accompanied her—but Gavin, determined to usurp Felicity's place in Lady DuFrayne's affections by fair means or foul, was doing what he could to reserve Aunt Agnes's attentions for himself. He therefore attached himself to every outing that involved Miss Pennington, including the visits to the Pump Room.

He could not hope to estrange the two women, and only a dastard would attempt to actually turn Aunt Agnes *against* Felicity...but at the very least, he could remind his redoubtable aunt of his own claim on her affections and, he hoped, pry her a little loose from Felicity's clutches. His aim, which was admittedly vague, was merely to scotch private conversations between Aunt Agnes and Felicity—and encourage his aunt to turn to him rather than to her niece for companionship.

On Thursday, he very nearly succeeded in spiriting Aunt Agnes to the Pump Room before Felicity arrived to join them. He actually had Lady DuFrayne out the door, on his arm, when she spied Felicity walking in their direction from Henrietta Street and pulled him to a halt.

"Ah," she said, with great satisfaction. "Here comes my goddaughter. We will wait for her, Gavin."

Felicity saw them stopping on the pavement and raised a gloved hand in greeting. Soured as his mood was by the sight of her, hastening to encroach on his time with their aunt, his mouth twisted in a reluctant smile when a stray sunbeam lit her up just as the wind caught at her, ruffling the feathers that crowned her hat and slapping the flap of her pelisse across her skirts. She made a graceful, pretty picture, he had to admit. She had clothed her tall, slender person in strong colors against the winter gloom, and carried herself with such easy confidence it was a pleasure just to watch her cross the street. She skimmed across Great Pulteney Street like a brightly-sailed brigantine, her dark red pelisse merrily snapping as the wind tugged at her.

As she walked up to them another gust of wind caught her and she placed one hand on her hat, looking up at Gavin with her brows arched. He misliked the gleam in her eye, attractive as it was. "Going without me?"

"You are so late, we thought you were not coming."

Aunt Agnes snorted. "Fustian! This jackanapes hurried me so, I nearly left the house without my cane."

He patted her hand. "You do not need the

cane, Aunt. You have my arm."

"She doesn't need the cane in any event," said Felicity. "Aunt Agnes is strong as an ox. She uses it because she thinks it gives her an air of distinction."

"And so it does," retorted their aunt. "Or would, had I any need of such tricks. Come along, Impertinence! It's too brisk to stand about."

"Where is Henry?"

"Indisposed. It seems he is coughing his lungs out in the servants' quarters. Ha! I've no patience with it."

Felicity opened her mouth to say something, evidently thought better of it, and hid a smile with her hand. Gavin supposed that she was thinking the same thing he was: Aunt Agnes herself had just conquered the same ailment, and had probably passed it to Henry. No point in mentioning it, of course.

"I offered to dance attendance on our aunt in Henry's place," he said.

"That's kind of you, Gavin." Felicity firmly took Aunt Agnes's arm and motioned him back with her hand. "Now step back and follow us, as a good footman ought."

Aunt Agnes's low chuckle sealed his fate. Drat the woman. Her wicked sense of humor led her to encourage Felicity's high-handed ways—and his own, to be perfectly fair. She just loved to watch sparks fly, and cared little who got singed in the process.

"Minx," he growled in Felicity's ear. Then he fell back a pace or two, as bade. He knew when he'd been bested. The two women immediately put their heads together and began a low-voiced conversation that he could not overhear—although he could hear Aunt Agnes snorting with laughter from time to time.

He realized he was clenching his teeth and

forced himself to relax his jaw.

The distance was short, but their progress was slow. As they approached the middle of the bridge, Lady DuFrayne's attention was caught by an acquaintance exiting a shop, and she halted to converse with her friend. Felicity seized this opportunity to give him a sly smile, her grey eyes sparkling with mischief. He stepped up and spoke to her in a low voice. "Are you laughing at me, saucebox?"

"Yes, as a matter of fact I am." The feathers on her hat danced jauntily in another gust of wind, and her impudent smile broadened. "I hope you don't think you are bamboozling our aunt. She is awake on every suit, you know."

"I don't know what you mean."

"Yes, you do." Felicity bit back a laugh. "You are trying to cut a wheedle. Oh, pray do not give me that wounded look! You are transparent as glass."

"I am merely trying to get reacquainted with my aunt. Only think how long I have been away!"

"A very long time, to be sure. Had you forgotten her?"

"By no means."

"Nor has she forgotten you. There is no need for you to stick to her like a burr on a buffalo."

He tried for an expression of dignified reproach. "I have never seen a buffalo."

"Nor have I, but evidently burrs stick to them with astonishing tenacity. Much the way you are clinging to our aunt."

He attempted to frown at her and found he couldn't. Chagrined, he glanced away—and saw a sight so surprising that his expression must have changed, for Felicity turned to follow his gaze. And together they stood—stock still—

contemplating the spectacle in shared amazement.

A lady and gentleman in a curricle were approaching at a spanking pace behind a very fresh, nervous-appearing young chestnut. What was astonishing was that the gentleman was Oliver Stanhope, leaning back against the squabs with a delighted grin on his face, and the lady was Lulu Pennington, eyes sparkling, face flushed—and driving. She sat bolt upright, handling the reins with no sign of hesitation or fear; in fact, she looked to be enjoying herself very much indeed. Her hat had blown off her head and was dangling behind her, hanging from her neck by its ribbons. Her blonde curls were falling from their careful arrangement and flying round her face in wisps. She was clearly having the time of her life, and concentrating so hard on her task that she did not see her family members standing on the pavement staring at her. She drove right past them with nary a glance and continued up Great Pulteney Street.

Gavin looked instinctively at Felicity, seeking clarification, but her expression surprised a laugh out of him. "You look even more astounded than I am. When did Lulu purchase a curricle?"

She choked, then cleared her throat. "Ah— it is Mr. Stanhope's curricle, I believe."

"You *believe?*"

She shrugged helplessly. "I suddenly find that I am no longer certain of anything, where Lulu is concerned. I thought..." her voice trailed off and her brows knitted.

"Yes?"

"Gavin," she said, in a different tone, "tell me. Would you say that a gentleman taking a lady out in his curricle and letting her drive it indicates a—a particular regard for that lady?"

140

He rubbed his chin thoughtfully. "Almost certainly. But it could be nothing stronger than friendship. It's hard to say." He grinned down at her. "I think I would let you drive my curricle, if I had one. It might be a vastly amusing way to spend a morning."

"I see." She lapsed into a pensive silence.

Aunt Agnes continued to the Pump Room on the arm of her friend, whose maid trailed behind them, so Felicity took Gavin's arm and they brought up the rear. Her brown study continued until they were passing the abbey.

"I've another question, if you don't mind," she said at last.

"My dear Felicity, I live to serve you. Ouch," he added, although he could barely feel her pinch through his coat sleeve.

"Pray be serious, for I was never more so! It occurs to me that Lulu appears more to advantage here in Bath—sledding and driving curricles and so forth—than she ever will in a London ballroom."

"She is a dreadful dancer," he agreed. "And not at her best in company, either."

"That is precisely what I mean. She is very much an out-of-doors creature. And although that would not appeal to every man, to a certain sort of man, it would. Do you think Oliver Stanhope is that sort of man? Because I begin to think he is."

He feigned astonishment. "Why, Felicity Pennington—are you matchmaking? For shame!"

"Pish-tosh!" she retorted, sounding very much like Aunt Agnes. "Of course I am. And if you know what is good for you, you will help me."

They had reached the entrance to the Pump Room. Gavin pulled her aside to continue their conversation in relative privacy.

"Tread carefully, Cousin," he warned her.

"Mr. Stanhope seems rather the country squire type—which would, on the face of it, suit Lulu down to the ground—but we have no right to interfere. Matchmaking schemes rarely succeed. And if we do succeed, we will be plagued with remorse if he turns out to be the wrong man for her after all. Neither of us knows him well."

"You can remedy that more easily than I." Gavin groaned, but Felicity seized his hands and leaned forward, speaking urgently. "I realize I am asking a great deal of you, but think! You have been chafing at the notion of our aunt spending her money—which we both know you wish was yours!—on a Season for Lulu. If Lulu contracts an eligible match right here in Bath, she need not go to London."

He winced. "Must you put it so baldly? My motives are not completely mercenary."

Her eyes twinkled. "No, but to the extent that they are, I do not blame you in the least. So let us speak plainly to each other."

"What, precisely, do you want me to do?"

"Befriend Mr. Stanhope."

He looked askance at her. "What if we don't like each other?"

"If you don't like him that will be valuable information, and we shall take it into account before moving forward."

"And if he doesn't like me?"

She laughed merrily. "Oh, Gavin! Everyone likes you."

He was suddenly aware that he still held both her hands, and had to quell an overpowering urge to kiss her. Felicity Pennington, of all women! He must be going soft in the head.

She either sensed some portion of what he felt—or felt, herself, that she had blurted out more than she meant to say. Her cheeks turned pink and she pulled her hands from his. "We should probably go inside," she said.

He winked and offered his arm. "I am touched, you know, that you have such faith in my power to charm."

This seemed to restore Felicity's equilibrium. She took his arm. "Well, don't puff up. If your head swells any larger than it already is, your hat will fall off."

## Chapter Thirteen

The approach of Christmas brought a whirl of festivities. Lady DuFrayne took Felicity and Lulu to the theater every Tuesday, and escorted her protegees to Monday dress balls and Thursday cotillions in the Assembly Rooms. Other evenings were filled with dinners and musicales, soirees and concerts. Days were for shopping, teas, visits to the Pump Room, and morning visits. The sisters also joined their aunt for her mornings at home, helping her to receive visitors. Felicity observed Lulu closely when she could, hoping that her sister would acquire easier manners as she became acquainted with more people. Unfortunately, as far as she could tell, Lulu remained shy and awkward around everyone—everyone, that is, except her own family and Oliver Stanhope. In Mr. Stanhope's presence, she bloomed like a rose. Since Felicity remained entirely in the dark as to Mr. Stanhope's intentions, she found this vexing.

Another niggling worry pulling at her was that Lulu did not appear to be making friends with any of the young women in her new circle. Or, more to the point, the well-bred young ladies of Bath—and their watchful mamas—seemed to be holding themselves aloof. She hoped she was imagining this, but unfortunately her worst suspicions were confirmed—at church, of all places, on the last Sunday of Advent.

The Penningtons always sat near the front of the nave with Lady DuFrayne. It generally took some time to exit the abbey from there, because at the conclusion of the service the aisle quickly filled as everyone moved toward the narthex—and then, inevitably, progress slowed to a crawl as churchgoers greeted each other on the way out. Felicity found herself standing in the midst of the crush, directly behind two young women whose hair and faces were obscured by their hats. She did not mean to eavesdrop, but could not help overhearing when one said, very clearly, to the other: "Miss Pennington I like very well, but I believe her sister is not quite the thing."

The words seemed to echo, buzzing, in the air. *Her sister is not quite the thing.* Then the two hats drew close together and the conversation dropped to a volume Felicity could no longer hear.

Her cheeks burned. Should she speak? As she wavered, too distressed to think quickly, the moment passed; Nora touched her sleeve and spoke to her, and the two girls melted into the crowd ahead.

*Not quite the thing.* An accusation so vague it was impossible to refute!

Felicity knew well how harmful such pronouncements could prove. There was nothing in Lulu's character or disposition to warrant social ostracism, but a lady's reputation was fragile. Once tarnished, however unjustly, it never shone as brightly as before. Were this London, where casual cruelty, rumor, or spite could toss a girl aside for any reason or no reason, a defenseless nobody like Lulu might have all her hopes dashed and never find out why. Here in Bath, however, she was not without friends.

Felicity's hands clenched into fists and her jaw set. *Not quite the thing.* "We'll see about that," she muttered.

"See about what?" said Gavin, materializing at her elbow like an unsummoned spirit.

"Nothing," she said crossly. "You have the ears of a bat."

"Dear me." He touched his ears self-consciously, his expression so quizzical that she smiled in spite of herself. "Your expression was quite murderous, Miss Pennington. Remember where you are."

She sighed. "You are right. I shall command my temper until I step outside the abbey doors. After that, I cannot promise anything."

When they reached the narthex, he gripped her elbow and drew her to one side, away from the doors. "Stay a moment," he said. "I would ask you to walk the square with me, but it's too cold for comfort. If we return to Laura Place with the others, we cannot speak privately. But I think a conversation in the abbey will raise no eyebrows. What ruffled your feathers?"

"A conversation in the abbey," she retorted.

"No! With whom?"

"Between whom. And I don't know." She told him the story, and had the satisfaction of seeing his brows contract into a frown as he listened. He knew as well as she the damage that malicious gossip could do.

"Miss Bliss has been busy, it seems," he said drily.

"Well, in charity, recall that she was not the only person who encountered Lulu in that cloakroom. There was at least one other lady with her."

"It is unlikely, however, that the other lady

146

also has designs on Mr. Stanhope."

"What has that to do with—" Felicity broke off, startled. "Do you suppose this gossip is driven by jealousy?"

"I do indeed." He glanced, seemingly casually, around the narthex as the throng of chattering churchgoers continued to flow out the doors, and lowered his voice. "From what I am told, Miss Bliss expects an offer of marriage from the young man in question, and his silence on the subject is making her a trifle anxious. And—also from what I am told—she has good reason to fear that he may never come to the point."

Felicity caught her breath. "Because of Lulu?"

He nodded. "Say nothing," he warned her.

"Of course not. But this is excellent! Thank you! You spoke with him directly, I take it?"

"It has been an easy task to befriend Mr. Stanhope. I like him."

"If Lulu secures his affections, gossip cannot touch her. I could even find it in me to pity Miss Bliss."

"We are not there yet, Cousin. Stanhope feels a keen sense of obligation to Miss Bliss. He has known her forever, and his family is urging him to make the match."

"Oh dear." Her heart sank. "I told Lulu as much, but she is too besotted to heed me. Should I try to keep them apart? I do not want her heart broken if I can prevent it."

He rubbed his chin. "Well, we are not there yet, either. On the whole, Lulu seems to be winning the contest, so if I were you I would give her free rein. Let her be around him as much as she can, and let her be herself. If she wins his heart, it will be well and truly won. If he acquires a distaste for her, better now than later."

She bit her lip, irresolute. "Your advice

sounds reasonable Gavin, but 'tis hard to watch her tumbling headlong into love with a man whom everyone expects to marry another."

"I'm sure it is. But I have an idea that could very well bring matters to a head."

"Really? What is it?"

He grinned at her, then laughed and shook his head. "I cannot tell you. Remember, I have befriended Stanhope! And now if I tell you the advice I gave him, I will betray his confidence. I never betray a friend's confidence."

"Gavin, really! You are an infuriating creature."

He clicked his tongue at her in mock sorrow. "Such a temper. No wonder you remain unwed."

She glared at him. "The wonder is that you remain unmurdered."

He laughed and pulled her arm through his. The crowd had thinned and they easily passed into the paved square fronting the abbey. As they turned toward Laura Place he chuckled again. "I like you, Felicity," he said. "Always have."

"Thank you," she said icily.

"I do think it odd, you know, that no one has offered for you. Why do you suppose that is?"

"Aunt Agnes tells me that the men today are all nincompoops."

He burst out laughing. Felicity felt an answering smile tug at her reluctant lips. She simply couldn't stay cross with him for longer than five minutes, it seemed. She sighed and patted his arm. "This unfortunate state of affairs doubtless accounts for the other peculiar circumstance," she said.

"What peculiar circumstance?"

She opened her eyes at him. "Why, the fact that no one has murdered you, of course."

"Because men are nincompoops?"

"And women are as soft-hearted as men are soft-headed." She shot him a darkling glance. "Beware the day when our well of charity runs dry."

"I am shaking in my boots. Will you and Lulu attend Mr. Stanhope's skating party on Tuesday?"

"Heavens, yes. Lulu talks of nothing else. Are you staying on for dinner as well? It should be a pleasant way to spend Christmas Eve."

"Yes, although changing clothes at someone else's house will be a nuisance."

She laughed. "I daresay if you sat down to dinner in your skating garb, Mr. Stanhope would scarcely notice. He has a strong taste for informality."

"Alas, Aunt Agnes will be present, so I dare not."

"Pudding-heart," she murmured provocatively.

"No such thing!" He looked pained. "I defer to her wishes from pure, disinterested courtesy."

At this point they caught up with the rest of the family and private conversation was at an end. Felicity was left with much to think about, and no one but Gavin to confide in. She wondered if this was the reason why her thoughts turned to him so often...for they surely did. Little as she trusted him, in this important matter he was her ally, her co-conspirator, and her only confidante. Perhaps it was only natural that she would think of him a dozen times a day or more.

Of course, when she was honest with herself, she had to admit she thought of him more often than was strictly necessary. In fact, she thought of him whenever her thoughts were not directly claimed by someone or something else. And no amount of self-scolding seemed able to banish his handsome, mocking image from her brain. It seemed quite clear what her New Year's Resolution would be. She must, she really *must,* stop mooning over Gavin DuFrayne!

On Tuesday morning she and Lulu carried their dinner dresses, packed in bandboxes with tissue between the folds, to Aunt Agnes's house. Skates dangled by their laces from the sisters' wrists like ridiculously heavy reticules. Lulu's blue eyes shone with excitement and her feet fairly danced; a day at Mr. Stanhope's house was her notion of heaven. Felicity sighed and shook her head at her, but could not help laughing a little, too, to see Lulu so happy over such a tiny thing.

They joined their aunt and Gavin for the drive to Westfield. Aunt Agnes's devoted Williams, a satchel balanced on her lap, sat inside the landau with Lady DuFrayne and the Pennington sisters, and Gavin's man Ashanti sat on the box beside the driver. Gavin rode beside them on a hired hack, so thickly wrapped against the cold in his greatcoat and muffler that he looked like a highwayman. Lulu's joy proved contagious and they made a merry party as they bowled toward their destination.

Oliver Stanhope woke in darkness on the day before Christmas, feeling such a high pitch of anticipation that further sleep was impossible. He toyed with the idea of ringing for light and hot water, but then he heard the hall clock faintly chiming six o'clock. It would be heartless to rouse the household two full hours before they expected him to be up. He lit his own fire, therefore, and dressed by the light of a single candle.

150

The room was arctic—which pleased him, because the cold snap had made his skating party possible. For the past week, he and his staff had been preparing the pond, sweeping the snow and debris from its surface and pouring barrels of water on it to freeze and refreeze until the thick surface shone smooth and glassy. In a clearing beside the pond, he and the male members of his staff had dragged wooden benches into a rough circle and caused a stone firepit to be built in the center, with corded wood stacked handily nearby. There was nothing like a sit-down by a fire and a hot drink when you were skating. If he were able thus to keep his guests refreshed, they might skate all day—or as long as the light lasted. He rubbed his hands together with delight, picturing the fun in store.

He had every expectation that the day would be pleasant, but skating was not the only— nor the most important—plan he had made. Restlessness as much as hunger drove him from his chamber and downstairs to the kitchen, where he found his cook directing two sleepy-looking girls from the village in rolling pastry. They stopped what they were doing to drop curtseys to him when he popped in, which he waved away with a laugh. "Don't let me interrupt you, or Mrs. Burr will have my hide," he told them, stealing a hot oatcake from a platter. "Whatever you are doing is far more important than—I say! These are first-rate."

"Thank you, sir," said Mrs. Burr, looking a trifle harassed.

"But I really came down here to see the greenery."

She nodded toward the scullery door. "Through there, if you please, sir. It's stacked in the mudroom, and some in the potting shed as well. Will you be wanting your breakfast early, then?"

"Whenever is convenient," he assured her. "I know you have much to do today."

"Yes, sir, the kitchen will be busy."

But Oliver was already through the door and heading to the mudroom, where the fragrance of fresh-cut boughs assailed his nostrils, bringing with it a thousand lovely memories. He inhaled deeply, smiling. "Christmas," he said, rubbing his hands together again. "Ha!"

A freckled face popped over the tallest stack of boughs. "Did you say something, sir?" piped Mrs. Burr's son.

"Not a word. How are you, Sam? Ready to hang the green?"

"Almost, sir—it's all been washed, just waiting for the girls to tie it up with ribbons and that. They'll be here any time now."

"Good. Good." It was unbelievably cold in the mudroom. Oliver blew on his hands to warm them and prowled round the stacks. He was pleased to find a large table standing beneath the window with little wooden hoops, red ribbons, a basket of small apples, and all the other necessary parts to make kissing boughs, all laid out in neat rows. Someone, it seemed—probably Mrs. Tipton—was highly organized. He saw holly, fir, ivy, laurel, rosemary...but where was the mistletoe?

"Ah—Sam?"

"Yes, sir?"

"I don't see any mistletoe."

"No, sir." Sam's tone was congratulatory. "The trees in your wood are very healthy, sir."

Something like panic fluttered in Oliver's breast. "But we must have mistletoe! You can't make a kissing bough without mistletoe."

"Kiss 'em under the holly," suggested Sam.

He broke off a green, spiky twig sporting several red berries and handed it to Oliver. "It'll work just as well, if they're willing."

"I daresay, but the point of the kissing bough is that you can kiss them whether they're willing or not!"

Sam looked puzzled. "Why would you want to kiss a girl who an't willing?"

"Because—" Oliver raked a hand through his hair, frustrated. Mistletoe kissing wasn't something he felt equipped to explain to a lad of twelve summers. "Never you mind," he said. "But we need mistletoe!"

He went back in the house to hunt for Mrs. Tipton and nearly ran into her in the passage outside the kitchen. When she heard his concern she patted his arm in a motherly gesture and chuckled. "Now, sir, when you know me better you'll trust me a little, I hope! The village girls are bringing mistletoe from the trees behind the chapel." He had a strong suspicion that if he stayed, she might actually tell him to run along, as if he were a troublesome child underfoot rather than the master of the house. He retreated before his dignity could suffer that particular blow.

By the time he had finished dressing and breakfasting, Westfield was filled with laughing girls and boys from the neighborhood, a small army recruited by the Tiptons for the cheerful task of hanging the green. Delicious smells wafted from the kitchen, housemaids scurried here and there, helping with the decoration and all the last-minute preparations, and Oliver himself helped to carry in the gigantic punchbowl he had borrowed for the occasion. It was set in the place of honor in the center of his dining room table, to hold lemonade for the first part of the day and negus later.

There was barely time to shoo the last of

the young helpers down to the servants' hall, where gifts and food awaited them, when his guests began to arrive. It was amazing, he thought happily, how greenery and ribbons and the fragrance of baking could transform a house. His home quickly filled with friends and family, and every face wore a smile. His mother was acting as hostess, and as Oliver mingled with the would-be skaters, directing them to follow him to the pond, she looked after those who remained behind to play parlor games. The plan for the day was a flexible one. His guests could stay in the house, come out skating, or go back and forth at will. Because tonight was Christmas Eve, most could not stay for all the festivities. Many, especially the families with children, were coming only for the skating.

In the midst of the cheerful hubbub, he could not help keeping one eye on the door and one ear open for the arrival of the DuFrayne party. He was reluctant to head to the pond without Sir Gavin and the Pennington sisters— one of the Pennington sisters in particular. He lingered in the hall, dawdling a bit, while servants carried parcels upstairs and his friends tended to their skates and scarves, preparing to head out. And it was thus that he spied Almeria Bliss standing beneath a kissing bough.

The bough was hung in the arch of his library door. Had she noticed it? Was she standing there deliberately? She looked a bit self-conscious—but then, she often did. Never mind; whether she expected it or no, it was time to act. He was at her side in two quick steps. "Almeria!" he said, sliding his arm round her waist. "Happy Christmas!" And he kissed her.

He had never kissed her before, and was not sure what to expect. Her lips met his readily enough, albeit briefly, and although she pretended to push him away and turned pink, he thought she seemed more pleased than offended. "Oliver!" she cried, as if scandalized by his behavior—but she was laughing even as she scolded him.

All around them, people laughed and cheered, and cries of "Mistletoe! Mistletoe!" rang out. Predictably, young girls shrieked and ran and boys chased and hooted, and all was bedlam for a minute or two. Oliver looked up and saw Lulu Pennington standing in the doorway and his heart seemed to bound in his chest. She was dressed for skating with her blonde curls tucked up under a modest little black hat, and she had donned a thick red coat that might have seen better days. A battered pair of skates hung from her wrist. She was not dressed to impress or allure, but to him she looked delicious. He wished with all his heart he could pull her under the mistletoe right now. He put that thought firmly from his mind, however, and left Almeria's side to welcome the DuFrayne party to Westfield. He felt that now, at last, the day could truly begin.

A group of twenty or more had come prepared to skate. As Oliver led the way through the frosty morning air, Sir Gavin caught up with him. "Well?" he said. "Miss Bliss looked rather pleased with herself just now. Did you already catch her under the mistletoe?"

Oliver grinned. "No need, my friend. She waited for me."

"Dear me. So much progress, and well before noon! I congratulate you."

"Premature! I'm only halfway to the post."

"If I were a betting man, I'd say you'll get there before Christmas."

They were laughing, but Oliver felt a flutter of nerves at the thought of completing his plan for today. It involved kissing Lulu Pennington, and somehow that seemed far more momentous and difficult than kissing Almeria Bliss. Was it because he had known her such a short time? It was doubtful that she would wait for him beneath the mistletoe as Almeria had so conveniently done. He had no idea how he would bring it about, but he must make it happen somehow. For one thing, DuFrayne would chaff him unmercifully if he failed. For another... he glanced over his shoulder at the cheerful party trudging behind him, and spotted her red coat and blonde curls somewhere in the middle. The very sight of her made him smile, and he easily finished his thought: He wanted to kiss her. He'd wanted to since the first time he met her, sopping wet on Lady DuFrayne's marble floor.

Thank God for mistletoe. Today would be the day.

## Chapter Fourteen

Lulu's happy morning would *not* be ruined by Almeria Bliss. It would not, it would not, it would not.

She had overheard Miss Bliss talking archly about "tomboys" and "hoydens," declaring that she had never been one—and Lulu was nearly certain she had been meant to overhear it. Miss Bliss had been very prettily dressed...unlike Lulu ... and was staying in the house while the "hoydens" went skating. Well! She was very glad Miss Bliss was staying behind. Felicity was going skating, and Felicity was above reproach. Lulu felt perfectly confident that there was nothing *hoydenish* about skating if her sister did it. Everyone would have a much better time if Almeria Bliss remained in the house.

At least Lulu would.

The morning was exceedingly cold but beautiful, with sunshine peeping through the clouds from time to time and lighting up the snow. It hadn't snowed for days, but more of it remained on the ground out in the countryside than in town. The party was a jolly one, with a nice mix of adults and children, and when they arrived at the pond a shout went up from the younger members of the group. Lulu clapped her hands, thrilled. It was perfect! A glassy oblong of ice stretched before them, nearly a hundred yards long. At one end the shore rose up to a fence, with a meadow or pasture beyond, but the rest of the pond was lined with trees. Off to their left, a fire crackled, ringed with wooden benches and tended by a freckle-faced boy and Mr. Ashanti. The fragrance of cocoa mingled with wood smoke. Oh, yes, it was perfect.

People headed for the benches, eager to put on their skates, but Lulu stopped beside Gavin's manservant. "Are you changing employers, Mr. Ashanti?" she asked. "Sir Gavin will be sorry to lose you."

To her surprise, he burst out laughing— something she had never seen an English servant do—and shook his head. "No, no, missy, I am a volunteer today. Mr. Stanhope is giving yet another party before he be finish wit' staffing his house. I am glad to come because I never see skating before." He chuckled again. "I t'ink I stay close to the fire."

His accent was hard to follow but his smile was infectious. She laughed with him. "Very wise, I'm sure. I hope you enjoy the day."

She found a spot on one of the benches and bent to put on her skates. By the time she had finished lacing them as tightly as she could, the fitful sunlight had vanished behind thick and seamless clouds. "Oh!" cried the girl sitting beside her, in a tone of disappointment. "I thought the day might turn sunny."

"This is better," said Lulu cheerfully, tucking her laces into the top of her skates. "Sunshine on ice hurts your eyes. And often it's a bit warmer when it's overcast, you know."

"Spoken like a right one." Mr. Stanhope, already wearing skates, had glided up and was smiling down at her. "I'm glad to see you in skates, Miss Pennington. I was afraid you might sit out this morning's entertainment."

"Not I," she exclaimed, laughing. "You must be thinking of someone else."

Mr. Stanhope's warm smile faltered. Lulu felt the color rush into her face. Her stupid tongue! But to her surprise he took her hand and briefly clasped it, murmuring something that sounded very like, "Impossible." And then he was gone, speaking to others as he moved among his guests, ensuring everyone felt welcomed and attended to.

*Impossible.* Had she heard him aright? Her heart swelled with dazzled happiness. *Impossible* for him to think of someone else! What could it mean but—

—but nothing. She might not have heard him correctly, and even if she had, she might be misinterpreting his words. Or, rather, word. A single word! It might mean anything.

Or it might mean something. The fizz of joy could not be repressed. And why, after all, should she try to tamp it down? Either Mr. Stanhope was going to marry Miss Bliss or he was not. If he were, today might be her last chance to enjoy his company with a whole and happy heart, and she would not ruin the day with nitpicking.

The ice stretched before her, smooth as glass, as yet unscored by the dozens of skates that were about to mark it. She laughed from pure pleasure, pushed off, and floated across its perfect surface like a bird in flight.

Felicity buried her hands in her muff and sighed. Now or never, she supposed. She stole a glance at the assortment of wooden chairs that had been assembled to assist children who were learning to skate, and wished she dared snag one for her own use. It wasn't that she couldn't skate. Of course she could skate.

She just couldn't skate well.

And Gavin knew it, the wretch. His own skates hissed as he pulled up before her with a flourish. "Hallo, Cousin, why so glum?"

"I am not your cousin," she informed him for the umpteenth time. "And I'm perfectly well, thank you."

"Do you mean to sit on that bench all morning?"

"I might." She lifted her chin at him. "I like it here."

"It's more fun out on the ice. Do you need a hand?"

"I don't *need* a hand," she said, with dignity. "I was just about to start skating, as a matter of fact." He grinned at her and she bit her lip. "Oh, very well. If you must know, I would feel more comfortable with someone steadying me."

He held out his hand, still grinning. She took it, but warily. "Not too fast, Gavin, I beg of you."

"Fear not," he said cheerfully. "I haven't signed up for any races yet."

She rose from the bench and clutched his arm. In so doing, she nearly dropped her muff. She teetered while attempting to catch it.

"Steady on," he said, helping her as she wrestled with the muff. "Here. Let's try this." He slipped one arm firmly round her waist. "You're better at dancing than skating. Pretend we are dancing."

"Oh," she said faintly. "Very well." She slipped her hands back in the muff, trying not to blush. Gavin held her in what could only be called an embrace. His left arm circled her waist, pulling her close in to him, and his right hand steadied her right elbow. It felt shockingly intimate, but she did feel less likely to fall.

She hoped the pose did not look as scandalous as she feared it did, but then she glanced rather anxiously into his face and was lost. His smile, now so near, and the warmth in his eyes undid her. She felt an answering smile rise in her and curl her lips, and suddenly she no longer cared how their skating pose looked. It felt marvelous.

"Right foot first," he said. "Just lean with me. Here we go."

*Dancing,* she reminded herself. And followed.

Oliver was too busy seeing to his guests to skate for his own pleasure. He mingled with the company, saw that the learners were supplied with chairs or stools to cling to for their first attempts to slide across the ice, ensured that Sam was stirring the cocoa enough to keep it from boiling, checked that the fire was burning briskly, the ice was strong, and everyone was smiling. Yet all the while he laughed and talked and busily dashed here and there, he was aware of Lulu Pennington. It was like she held a string tied around his heart and whatever he did and wherever he went, he sensed its pull. He felt impatient to get to her—to reach the moment when he could, without attracting undue notice, skate by her side and bask in her company.

From the corner of his eye he saw her again and again. Lulu helping the little ones skate, Lulu flying across the ice with a group of laughing girls, Lulu playing jump-the-hat, Lulu perched on a bench with her hands cupping a mug of chocolate as she breathed in the steam. He dared not go to her for fear that everyone present would witness the way she made him feel. And yet she drew him, irresistibly. He had finally arrived at a point when it seemed to him that everyone was busy at last and he could follow his own inclinations, when his brother James skated purposefully toward him.

"A word with you, Oliver," he said.

He stifled his disappointment and managed to smile. "Hallo, James. Beautiful skating weather, isn't it?"

"Yes." James was not smiling. "I hope you don't mind a bit of brotherly advice."

"About the weather?" He tried to speak lightly, but did not suppose it would have any effect. And it didn't. James's expression was troubled, and he ignored Oliver's flip rejoinder.

"I don't mean to intrude on your affairs, but I think you may not be aware of something—something that concerns you nearly."

It was unlike James to be so direct. He must be deeply moved. Oliver's smile faded. "What is it?"

"I fear that tongues have been wagging. I have reason to think that..." He looked uncomfortable and lowered his voice. "It's awkward to speak about such matters, and I daresay it's none of my business, but I thought you should know. There are those who believe you are showing a decided preference for Miss Lulu Pennington. You and I know it must be nonsense, but I thought I would put you a little on your guard. I am sure you do not want to injure Miss Pennington in any way."

"Ah. Oh. I see." Annoyance and chagrin nearly choked him. Hang it all! Why must people be so everlastingly interested in matters that did not concern them? Why couldn't a man be left in peace to make up his own mind? "That is awkward," he managed to say. "No, I would not injure Miss Lulu for the world."

"Nor Almeria, I am sure."

"Certainly not."

A faint smile lightened James's sober countenance. "I saw you kiss her this morning, and others saw it as well. Perhaps that will put a stop to the worst of the gossip."

"Oh, well, as to that—it was a mistletoe kiss. There's nothing in a mistletoe kiss."

James's smile vanished. "Oliver, you cannot kiss a lady without declaring your intentions. Or at the very least, your preference for her."

"You can at Christmastime." Impatience sharpened his tone. "A kiss under the mistletoe is part of the fun. It has no more meaning than— than dancing with a lady." Although, he had to admit, kissing Almeria had given him considerably more information than dancing ever had.

James frowned. "I do not know if Almeria's view comports with yours. She may think you are on the verge of a declaration."

Oliver snorted. "I daresay she does. She has thought that for years, I am told."

"And are you?"

This was blunt indeed. Oliver looked at him in surprise. "Does it matter?"

"Yes, it does." James seemed to be laboring under strong emotion. "I do not resent our grandfather making you his heir. You are the only one of us who is following a secular path. You were, therefore, the logical choice to purchase an estate and set up a household. But this means that your choice of a wife affects the future of our entire family, far more than my own choice, or

Charles's, will do."

"Why, then, I will tell you. I am on the verge of a declaration—I think. But I will not take such a serious step until I am perfectly sure what I want." His eyes traveled involuntarily to a girl on the ice...a girl whose blonde curls were tucked under a little black hat.

James turned to follow Oliver's gaze and a strange sound escaped him. He turned back to his brother. "Is the gossip true, then?"

He jammed his hands in his pockets, wishing it weren't necessary to admit it. But James had a right to know. "It would be true, if Almeria were not in the picture. A man does not lightly turn his back on the wishes of his family and the expectations of an old friend, merely to..." He sighed. "Indulge an infatuation."

"Is that what this is?"

"I don't know. It's something I have never felt before."

He was not in the habit of confiding in James. He loved his brothers, of course, but they were so different from himself that they had little in common apart from their familial bonds. Still, they had grown up together and he supposed, in his way, James knew him better than anyone else on earth. James knew Almeria, too, so he might be uniquely positioned to advise him.

"Tell me what you would do," he said impulsively. "You know the way I am. I cannot picture a life with a woman like Almeria. I have tried, but my imagination fails me. I think she might make me unhappy. Worse, I think I might make her unhappy."

James spoke slowly. "Almeria is a woman of intelligence and breeding. She has a sterling reputation and an affectionate heart."

"But not a merry one."

The two men stared at each other in

silence. James's expression indicated that he was wrestling with the notion of a merry heart being an important quality in a wife. To him, it would not be, Oliver knew. It might be hard for him to see it from Oliver's point of view.

"You have honored me with your confidence, and I will not abuse it by scolding you." A faint smile lifted the corners of James's mouth. "We all hoped that Almeria's influence might settle you down a bit."

Oliver laughed long and hard. His brother looked sheepish. "I don't know why you find it funny. Marriage often has a sobering effect."

"Heaven forbid!" Oliver shook his head, still laughing. "You see I am a hopeless case. Truth be told, Almeria's notions of propriety are too strict for me. I would drive her mad with my fast horses and large parties and free-and-easy ways. She might be a better match for you, brother—she would make an excellent vicar's wife."

He was joking, but to his surprise James's face turned red. "I'll not deny that the thought has occurred to me."

Oliver's jaw dropped. "No! Is this why you're dragging me over the coals? By Jove, man—why didn't you say as much? I thought you were dangling after Miss Pennington."

James's expression turned gloomy. "Mother mentioned her and thought she might do for me. She's a very good sort of girl, not too young, not flighty. She has a good head on her shoulders. Well-connected." He heaved a sigh. "But I fear she is strong-minded." He looked past his brother's shoulder and frowned. "And not as careful about appearances as I would like."

Oliver turned and saw Miss Pennington skating with DuFrayne. The rascal had her pulled tight against his body as he steered her around the pond. To be fair, Miss Pennington appeared to be not a strong skater, but really...the picture they made was not designed to recommend itself to his strait-laced brother. He coughed and hid a smile behind his hand. "I see. It seems that Mother's matchmaking skills do not equal her genius for embroidery."

"Ha. Very true."

They stood in silence for a few moments, watching Felicity Pennington wobble across the ice clinging to DuFrayne, and Lulu Pennington dreamily practice figure eights in the center of the pond as the other skaters zipped past her.

"Do you suppose it would be enough for Mother if one of us courts Almeria Bliss and the other courts a Pennington girl? It wouldn't be precisely the matches she had in mind, but she could still declare victory and retire from the field triumphant."

This sally coaxed a smile from James. "There is no guarantee I would succeed."

"I am not certain of success, myself. But I think we should take a stab at it. It strikes me that I am more likely to be happy with Lulu Pennington than Almeria, and you are more likely to be happy with Almeria than Felicity Pennington."

Another silence fell. Oliver glanced at his brother. James seemed to be lost in thought. He cleared his throat. "If things go the way I hope they will go, Almeria may need some consoling. You could, ah, leap into the breach."

James frowned. "And if things don't go the way you hope they will go, what then? Will you offer for Almeria? She is clearly ready to accept you."

He took a deep breath of the clean, frosty air and expelled it, smiling. Suddenly one thing, at least, seemed to come into focus. Of this, he was—at last—quite sure. "I am not the man for

Almeria Bliss. I intend to press my suit with Lulu Pennington. If my suit is unsuccessful, I will be no more the man for Almeria than I am now. That ship has sailed." He clapped his brother on the back. "I wish you good fortune."

He headed for the center of the pond with a lighter heart than he had enjoyed in many weeks.

## Chapter Fifteen

Lulu saw Oliver Stanhope skating toward her and abandoned her attempt to close the circle on a figure eight. To reach her, he had to dodge people who were skating round the perimeter of the pond, and was breathless by the time he met her in the center. "You choose a dangerous spot to practice your figures, Miss Pennington," he said, laughing.

She waved her arm in a gesture that encompassed the entire pond. "It is only dangerous to get here, not to be here. Once you reach the center, you are quite alone."

"And do you like to be alone, Miss Pennington?"

She started to laugh, but the laugh died on her lips when she saw the earnestness of his expression. He was smiling, but there was something in his eyes that caught her, throwing her off-stride. "Alone? I...ah...no. Not particularly," she stammered.

"I am glad to hear it." He glanced around the pond, almost self-consciously, then offered her his arm. "Would you care to skate with me?"

Her morning was now complete; there was nothing more it could offer. Blissfully happy, Lulu took Mr. Stanhope's arm and joined the throng of skaters circling the pond. Since everyone was traveling at a different rate of speed, navigating the circumference took a bit of skill—but skill, she soon learned, the two of them had in abundance. She was thrilled to discover that Mr. Stanhope's preferred skating style was nearly as boisterous as her own, and he matched her stride for stride. When they discovered they were kindred spirits in this, as in so many other things, they darted around and through groups of slower skaters, raced each other, and ended up nearly flying off the end of the pond, whooping with delight.

Mr. Stanhope grabbed both her hands at the edge of the ice and spun her back to the center. "You are a wonderful skater," he exclaimed. "Better than I am, I think! Where did you learn? Not in Bath, I'll warrant."

"No—Kent! My uncle Jasper taught me. Lady DuFrayne's late husband, you know." She was panting and had to stop for breath. "Whew!"

He grinned at her. "Uncle Jasper must have been a right one."

"Oh, yes—he was the best of uncles. We spent Christmases at Ashwood Hall when he was alive, and had some wonderful skating when I was a little girl. My sisters never cared for it as much as I did." She looked around for Felicity and did not see her. Gavin was skating with Miss Steele now. Lulu giggled. "As you see! Felicity has gone back to the house. Half an hour is as much skating as she can bear."

The number of skaters waxed and waned as people went back and forth from the house to the pond, or sat on the benches by the fire to warm up, drinking chocolate. But Lulu and Mr. Stanhope stayed out on the ice for the next hour, skating companionably and talking, too absorbed in each other's company to notice the time passing. Lulu told him tales of Uncle Jasper that made him shout with laughter, and she confided, rather wistfully, that she missed him still. "He truly loved children. I believe he spent more time with us than he did with his adult guests! He certainly seemed to have more fun chasing us across the lawn than attending to his duties as host. 'Twas a pity that he and Aunt Agnes never had children of their own."

"Who was Sir Gavin's father?"

Lulu wrinkled her nose. "Uncle Monty. We called him uncle, although he was Uncle Jasper's brother and not really an uncle to us girls. I don't think he liked us any more than we liked him. But all the DuFraynes resented us, you know. Except for Uncle Jasper." She laughed. "We came to Ashwood every Christmas, and stayed every summer as well. How it put their noses out of joint! I didn't understand it when I was little, of course, but now I see quite clearly. The entire family was hanging on Uncle Jasper's sleeve. They hated it that he loved his wife's family as if we were his own. Well! I daresay they were right to resent us, for only look how it ended! He left his entire fortune to Aunt Agnes —every farthing, except for the estate, which is entailed. I believe his sisters and Uncle Monty were furious."

She suddenly realized she was telling tales out of school and bit her lip, casting an anxious glance into Mr. Stanhope's handsome face. "I am sorry—I should not rattle on."

His smile, however, was as warm as ever. "I like to hear you rattle."

She blushed. "Really, Mr. Stanhope, you should not encourage me. My tongue runs away with me sometimes, and I say far more than I ought."

He nodded solemnly. "You are not discreet. But I am suspicious of discreet people, aren't you? They might be hiding something shameful. For if they were, who would know?" He shook his head in mock sorrow, which made her laugh again.

"Very true! At least with me, one always knows, for I cannot keep myself from—" She stopped, vexed with herself, and blushed again. "But we are talking nonsense," she said quickly. "Would you mind taking me back to the benches, Mr. Stanhope? I think I should tighten my laces."

She expected him to take leave of her once she was seated by the fire—after all, he had other guests who deserved his attention. But to her surprise, he sat beside her, tightening the laces on his own skates and telling her of his plans for Westfield. She listened with interest and applauded all of it; she told him it sounded delightful—which it did—from the building of an orangery to recarpeting the dining room. It was clear that Mr. Stanhope took pride in his new home and was looking forward with great enthusiasm to putting his own stamp on the place, and whatever interested Mr. Stanhope interested Lulu.

They stayed by the fire for some time, talking easily of this and that. It seemed the most natural thing in the world that he confided so many of his plans to her, and even asked her opinion from time to time. It was only when she noticed a certain speculative look on the face of the boy handing out the cocoa that she realized it was, perhaps, a bit odd of him to confide in her. The boy was casting furtive glances her way and doing his best to look impassive—which told her far more than if he had stared outright.

Lulu's heart beat faster, and she lost the thread of what Mr. Stanhope was saying. She held out her hands to the fire, which gave her an excuse to tear her eyes from Mr. Stanhope's fascinating face and look into the flames while she regained her composure.

But it seemed Mr. Stanhope was as attuned to her as she was to him. "What's amiss?" he asked.

"N-nothing. I was only..." She hesitated. "I was thinking that I have stolen too much of your time today. I am not your only guest. I fear we are...perhaps..." Her voice trailed off. She folded her hands in her lap and stared down at them. "I would not want people to think..." She bit her lip, unable to finish her sentence.

He finished it for her. "I am growing too particular in my attentions."

He sounded very grave. She glanced up at his face, frightened. The last thing she wanted to do was to hurt his feelings! "Oh, no! I am sure you are not. I know you would never behave ungentlemanly. But people are so mischievous, you know—at least in Bath—people will talk about any thing."

"You are right."A log in the fire before them popped and fell, sending up sparks that danced and whirled in the frosty air. The sky had turned leaden, bringing an early twilight. "It is selfish of me to spend so much time with you, merely because I enjoy it."

She could not help smiling. Whatever the future held, she would remember this day forever, and cherish the moment when Oliver Stanhope— best of men!—said that he enjoyed her company.

She smiled, but said nothing. Oliver studied her face with some anxiety, searching for clues. She had turned her face away from him and was looking at the fire. The curve of her cheek, while sweet to behold, told him little—except that she smiled.

At this tense moment he heard a soft cough and looked up. Mr. Ashanti had approached, and he had been too absorbed in studying Lulu Pennington to notice. Ashanti bowed. "Beg pardon, sir, but should we prepare to go in now?"

"Go in?" He looked around as if waking from a trance. The sky had darkened considerably and looked ready to spit snow at any moment. His pond was so deeply scored by hours of skating that the three or four boys who remained on the ice were having a tough go of it, although they still gamely chased each other and shouted. Everyone else had obviously gone back to the house. "Oh. Ah—yes, I suppose we should. Thank you, Ashanti." He tugged at his muffler, straightening it, and stood. "Before the light fails, I'd like you and Sam to get Tipton and the rest and pour water across the pond to refresh the ice. I've promised my staff a skating party on Boxing Day, and after all their hard work to make the ice perfect for today, we've ruined it. I'd like them to have as much fun as we had. You're invited for Boxing Day as well, of course—and any friend you'd care to bring." He skated over to the box where everyone's shoes were lined up, and grabbed his own—and the sole pair of ladies' shoes that remained, since they must, perforce, belong to Miss Pennington—and returned to his place on the bench. "It seems we tightened our laces to no purpose, Miss Pennington," he said with a smile, handing her her shoes.

"Yes. But oh, it was a lovely day!"

"It was, wasn't it? I am glad you think so too."

They busied themselves in removing their skates. Oliver wracked his brain to think what he ought to do next. The instant they returned to the house, all privacy would be at an end. His duties as host would demand that he attend to all his guests, not focus on Miss Lulu. He fancied it would not be difficult to catch her under the mistletoe at some point, but his heart quailed at the thought of kissing her so publicly. He did not want their first kiss—perhaps, if matters went awry, their only kiss—to be a hurried, jocular affair, part of a rollicking evening of Christmas games and festivities. Kiss Lulu for the first time—before an audience? No, the very idea was abhorrent!

He must screw his courage to the sticking point, then, and manage, somehow, to kiss her between here and the house. Suddenly his collar felt uncommonly tight. He cleared his throat and loosened his muffler a tad. Sam and Mr. Ashanti would be occupied for some time yet in dousing the fire, clearing away the chocolate, biscuit trays, and all the cups and utensils that had been used. The coast, therefore, was clear. He rose and offered his arm to Miss Pennington. She rose and took it.

"'Ware the ice," he cautioned her, pulling her close to his side. "It feels strange, doesn't it, to be back in shoes instead of skates?"

"Th-thank you," she stammered. "It does." And she clung to his arm in a most gratifying way.

He slowed his steps and they crossed the ice with caution. But when they reached the path that led through the woods to his house, and were walking on perfectly dry ground, he continued to pull her to his side...and she continued to hug his arm...and neither of them increased their pace. By mutual consent, then, they clung to each other and drifted like sleepwalkers beneath the overhanging trees. The warm lights of Westfield were visible ahead, but here, on the quiet path, they were alone. And Oliver knew his moment had arrived.

He drew her to a halt at the side of the path and took her hands. She seemed surprised, but did not pull away. Her blue eyes lifted to his, questioning—then dropped, seemingly transfixed by his topmost coat button. Color suffused her face—and still she did not pull away. Oliver's heart beat faster.

"Miss Pennington," he said. His voice sounded strangely hoarse. He cleared his throat. "I have a confession to make."

"Do you?" She seemed to be addressing his button. And her voice was no steadier than his own.

"Yes." How sweet she was, with her eyes downcast and her cheeks so pink! "I intended, from the moment I sent out the invitations to this party, to kiss you under the mistletoe today." Her lips parted in a soundless gasp. "In fact, it was the central feature of my planning."

"H-how extraordinary."

And still she did not pull away!

"I have changed my mind, however."

"Oh." Was that disappointment he sensed? Or merely confusion? And then she lifted those blue, blue eyes to his again and whispered, daringly, "Why?"

Time slowed to a dreamy crawl. A single snowflake drifted down and landed on her collar. He knew he would remember this moment forever. He wanted to touch her face—but not while wearing cold gloves. He wanted to kiss her *now*—but not before he answered her question. He wanted to hold her in his arms forever. That, at least, he would begin at once. He let go her hands and took her in his arms. And still, *still,* she did not pull away.

"Because," he told her hoarsely, "kissing you is not a game to me."

Her gloved fingers curled around his collar and her expression turned adorably saucy. "But Mr. Stanhope," she murmured, "what of my reputation? A lady needs a sprig of mistletoe to safeguard her character."

With his left hand, Oliver rummaged briefly in his greatcoat pocket and withdrew the sprig of holly Sam had given him that morning. He held it solemnly aloft. "This, Miss Pennington, will have to do."

And just as Sam had suggested, he kissed her under the holly.

## Chapter Sixteen

Gavin was standing in the hall, adjusting the placement of his stick pin before the oval mirror, when Mrs. Stanhope entered from the parlor. She checked when she saw him. "Oh, Sir Gavin, it is you! I beg your pardon. I thought my son Oliver had come in at last."

The poor lady looked rather harried. Gavin bowed. "Not yet, ma'am."

A burst of laughter from the parlor behind her, and the sound of music from the library behind him, bore testament to the fact that the party was going well. Many of the guests had taken leave of their hostess by now, however, and she was doubtless a trifle put-out by the continued absence of the host. Oliver Stanhope knew that the majority of his friends were not staying for dinner. He ought to have been on hand to bid his guests farewell, but he had yet to return from the skating pond. The clock had chimed four o'clock twenty minutes ago, it was quite dark outside, and a light snow was falling. Gavin himself had had ample time to change from his skating clothes into his dinner clothes, and others of the guests who were staying for dinner had disappeared above stairs to rest and change clothes as well. Doubtless Mrs. Stanhope desired to relinquish her duties and join them.

"I would go in search of him, had I not imprudently changed my clothes already," said Gavin, indicating his attire with an apologetic gesture. "The clothes I skated in were wet—"

"Oh, heavens, pray do not apologize," said Mrs. Stanhope, managing to smile—although with visible effort. "How absurd. It is not your duty to find my son! I daresay he will turn up at any moment. It is just so unlike him—"

At that moment she was interrupted by a group of departing guests who came in from the parlor to thank her, wish the Stanhope family a happy Christmas, and take leave. Gavin, feeling a bit self-conscious in his dinner attire, retreated to the back of the hall and slipped into the vestibule beyond. It led to the back door through which everyone had gone to and fro between the house and the skating pond, so he was in excellent position to witness Oliver Stanhope at last returning to Westfield—with Lulu Pennington on his arm. Both of them emitted a suspicious glow of happiness.

He was glad that he had thought to bring his quizzing-glass—which he had done precisely because he anticipated a moment like this! He raised the glass to his eye, drew himself up, and examined the blissful couple before him through its lens. "Dear me," he drawled. "We had quite given you up, Stanhope. How glad I am to see that you were not, after all, eaten by wolves."

Stanhope, in his present dazzled state, seemed impervious to chaffing. He merely grinned—although he did turn red. "Not as many wolves in these parts as there used to be, DuFrayne. But thank you for your concern."

Gavin bent his gaze—still magnified by the quizzing-glass—upon his friend's trousers and coughed. "Ahem! I spy a peculiar blot upon your right knee, Stanhope. Is it mud?"

Stanhope looked startled. He glanced down, turned even redder, and brushed futilely at the telltale spot. "Ah—it might be. Yes, it very well might be mud."

"And on your right knee only, I perceive. Good heavens, man. It looks almost as if you have gone down on one knee very recently. Yes..." He leaned closer, pretending to examine the stain with scholarly interest. "Yes, I would say you have knelt in the snow. Rather dirty snow. Since I feel quite certain that you would not, of course, kneel in mud."

"Not deliberately, at any rate."

"I am glad to hear it."

"Although one tends to be distracted at such a moment."

Gavin straightened in time to observe his friend grinning fatuously at Lulu, who put both hands over her mouth in an unsuccessful attempt to stifle a giggle.

He pretended to sniff the air. "Extraordinary. Here we are in the depths of December, and yet I catch a distinct whiff of April and May."

Lulu laughed outright at this. "Oh, Gavin, give over, do!" she begged. "You are putting me to the blush."

He grinned and, with a flourish, put his quizzing glass away. "Very well! Am I to wish you happy, Stanhope?"

"If you please. Although I cannot imagine feeling any happier than I am tonight."

Gavin bowed. "Then I shall wish you many years of feeling just this happy, and no more."

Stanhope wrung his hand, Lulu kissed his cheek, and Gavin dropped his mask of affectation and gave them to understand how truly glad he was about the match. Then Lulu went up on tiptoe and whispered something to Stanhope. He whispered back. She nodded, and slipped away into the hall.

"I sent her upstairs. She'll likely find her sister there, won't she?"

"I believe so." Gavin lifted an eyebrow at his friend. "I'm afraid you have a difficult conversation ahead of you."

Stanhope nodded, looking solemn. "I shan't put it off. Almeria deserves to hear the news from me, not through gossip." The besotted grin tugged at his mouth again. "And I am too happy to keep a sober face tonight, so I fancy the news will spread quickly."

"Poor Miss Bliss! I don't envy you the task."

"No, but I have reason to believe she will soon find consolation." Stanhope winked.

"Really! You astonish me."

He laughed. "I can't tell you who I have in mind for her, but I will confide this much: When I learned of his desire to take my place in her affections, I felt as if the weight of the world were lifted from my shoulders. Whew! I am still a bit giddy from relief."

"On several fronts, I fancy."

"Yes indeed!" Stanhope clapped him on the back. "I have to thank you, DuFrayne. Your idea was an excellent one."

Gavin laughed. "Now that the thing is done, I can tell you that I guessed how it would end."

Felicity smoothed the front of her red silk gown. Festive, she decided. And it looked well with her dark hair. Normally a single woman would not wear such a strong color—or expose so much of her bosom. But after all, it was Christmas Eve, and she was no longer a debutante.

She leaned toward the glass to slip the sparkling diamonds Aunt Agnes had lent her through her earlobes. Suddenly the door to the dressing room flew open and Lulu rushed in. One look at her sister's face, reflected in the mirror, told all. Felicity turned with a gasp.

"No!" she cried involuntarily, pressing one hand to her heart.

"Yes!" cried Lulu, and burst into happy tears. She was so overcome by joy, relief, and amazement that she could scarcely relate the story, but Felicity managed to decipher it at last. By the time the tale was completely told, they were seated side-by-side on a low bench against the wall of the makeshift dressing room Stanhope had set aside for the ladies. "Oh, Felicity—I have creased your dress."

"Never mind. I shall ask Williams to press it again; there is plenty of time before dinner. But, Lulu—are you really engaged to be married?"

Lulu nodded, sniffling. "As close as makes no odds. Oliver will speak to Mama tomorrow. Oh, I am the luckiest of women!" And her eyes filled again.

"Lulu, for pity's sake, do not cry!" Felicity dabbed her sister's eyes, laughing a little. "You must not ruin your looks before dinner. Many eyes will be upon you."

"Oh! Yes." She gulped. "I did not think of that."

Felicity rose, crossed to the door of the adjoining room, tapped on it once, and opened it. "Ah, Williams, there you are," she said drily. For Williams stood directly on the other side of the door, looking ridiculously guilty. She had obviously been listening to the sisters' conversation. It would not do to show it, but Felicity could not find it in her heart to blame her. Such exciting news was rare in the household. "I wonder if you could assist us? As you can see, my sister is still in her skating attire, and my dress, unfortunately, needs to be touched again with a hot iron."

"Yes, Miss," said Williams primly. "Lady DuFrayne is still resting, so I am at leisure to help you."

Felicity knew it was Williams's way of reminding her that she was not in the employ of the Pennington sisters. She had learned, over the past few years, to ignore the tiny slights doled out by her aunt's senior staff. But tonight's events gave her pause. She waxed pensive as she watched Williams help Lulu out of her bedraggled skating outfit. Lulu's marriage would increase the stature of the entire family. Well, not Aunt Agnes, of course—but Aunt Agnes would no longer be their sole claim to the notice of society. Lulu had made a respectable match. Almost a brilliant match. As mistress of Westfield House and daughter-in-law of Bishop and Mrs. Stanhope, Lulu's place in Bath would be firmly established among its most prominent residents.

And Lulu had no more notion of it than a babe in arms. She smiled affectionately as she watched Lulu sponge-bathe in her shift and slip into a fresh petticoat. Her sister's adventurous spirit and shining innocence had won her the affection of a truly worthy man, and Lulu was likely to be a happy woman. She would not give tuppence for what Bath thought of her—or London, for that matter—as long as she held the heart of Oliver Stanhope in her tender clasp. Felicity was nearly certain that Lulu had not even glanced around the room she was in to think how soon it would be hers, or what she might do with it. The thought made her chuckle, and Lulu looked at her inquiringly.

"Nothing, dearest. I am merely thinking how happy you will be."

Lulu's face lit up. Then she glanced at Williams, blushed, and returned her attention to her toilette.

Williams's true genius was for dressing hair, and Lady DuFrayne gave her talents little scope, so although she begrudged the Pennington girls assistance with their clothing she was happy to wield the curling iron and pins on their behalf. When Lady DuFrayne rose from her nap to be dressed for dinner and Williams hurried off to assist her, the sisters stood before the cheval glass and admired the picture they made. Lulu's platinum curls fell artlessly from a sort of topknot, and Felicity's smooth, dark locks had been crafted into an elaborate crown of braids, puffs, and ringlets in the latest mode, threaded with gold wire that caught the light. Lulu looked every inch the innocent she was, in pale blue ornamented with satin ribbons. Felicity looked like a French fashion plate, tall and slender in red silk with jewels glittering at her throat and ears.

"How sweet you look," said Felicity.

"How elegant you look," said Lulu. "No one would take us for sisters!"

"No," said Felicity with a sigh. "You look like Mama, and I like Papa—including the beak." She tapped her nose ruefully. "I am glad Aunt Agnes has it as well, or I would feel positively freakish. Run downstairs, now—you look very pretty. I will speak to Aunt Agnes."

Lulu looked relieved, and blew her sister a grateful kiss as she slipped out the door. Felicity pulled long white gloves to her elbows, sighed, and went into the adjoining room, where Williams was pinning Lady DuFrayne into her gown. As

Aunt Agnes declared that the room was too small to admit three women, she had to wait until her aunt was seated at the dressing table in the larger room, having her hair dressed, before she could tell her the news. Apart from lifting one brow and pursing her lips, Aunt Agnes showed little surprise.

Felicity pressed her a little. "It is an excellent match, is it not?"

"It is," said Lady DuFrayne. "I must own that you were right, and I was wrong. Lulu has done quite well for herself. She has spared me the botheration of taking her to London, too. Shall I cement the match tonight, standing *in loco parentis*? Ten to one your mother will make a mull of it, if it's left to her."

"Oh, as to that, all she need do is consent."

Aunt Agnes snorted. "Tut! Consent is only half the bargain. Tell your mother to send young Oliver to me for the settlements."

"Settlements? I had not thought—"

"No, you had not thought. Why should you? But marriage is a contract, my dear, and like any contract it must have terms." Aunt Agnes patted her coiffure. "One more pin here, I think, Williams."

"But Lulu has nothing to settle!"

"Your father left his girls a little something, did he not? Not enough, by any measure, but I might—if anyone were to ask me—supplement it a trifle. Never mind, Felicity, it is not your affair. I shall discuss it with your mother and the Stanhopes." She rose from the table and took up her cane. Upon seeing Felicity's expression, she chuckled and patted her cheek. "Surprised you at last, I see! Now let us go down to the parlor, or whatever young Stanhope calls it, before Lulu makes a cake of herself and ruins everything. I hope she will have a proper drawing room once

184

she is mistress here. Parlor! Faugh! I've no patience with it."

Chapter Seventeen

Felicity felt a little melancholy. She had slipped away from the rest of the party, ostensibly to visit the ladies' cloakroom, but now she lingered in the cold, dark hall to indulge the blue-devils for a few moments. There was nothing more exhausting than forced merriment. Her face hurt from smiling. Her head swam from drinking toasts.

She found, however, that standing alone in the darkness while light, warmth, music and laughter spilled from the adjacent library, echoed and intensified her sadness. It seemed a metaphor. Lulu's happiness was wonderful to behold, and naturally she rejoiced for her sister, but... but what? What was the matter with her?

Perhaps it was Christmas itself that depressed her spirits. Ever since Papa died, the holy day was bittersweet to her. But tonight, whatever the reason, she felt that all the light and warmth, all the music and laughter, was always in another room... surrounding others, enjoyed by others. However much she loved those happy people and longed for happiness herself, she stood apart, separated from all that made life meaningful. She was an onlooker, excluded from joy for reasons she did not understand.

A shadow moved in the doorway across from her and Gavin's voice said, "Felicity? Are you well?"

She cleared her throat. How silly, to be fighting tears over nothing! "Perfectly, thank you."

He moved toward her. "I was afraid you had gone home, like Miss Bliss, with a violent headache."

"Poor girl," said Felicity in a low tone. "I pity her." It was an excellent reminder, she told herself firmly, that others were facing worse heartache than she. Dean Bliss and his family had not stayed for dinner. They had taken Almeria away rather than force her to witness Mr. Stanhope and Lulu beaming and blushing.

"I daresay she'll come about. But what are you doing?"

She chuckled. "Moping. Pray laugh at me, Gavin, for I deserve it. I am standing out here feeling sorry for myself, and in truth, this melancholy is my own fault. All I need do is walk into the library to be surrounded by friends. Yet here I stay, cold and lonely."

"What a goosecap you are," he said, but his voice was warm with affection. "Here, let us go into the parlor. You can mope there in more comfort. The fire is still lit."

"I can't properly feel sorry for myself if you insist on making me comfortable." But she followed him into the parlor and watched him poke the fire back into life. He lit a couple of lamps, too. "You've ruined everything," she complained. "Now I feel positively cheerful."

"So do I," he said. He certainly looked pleased with himself. "May I tell you a secret?"

"A secret! How delicious. Of course you may."

He lowered his voice. "I'm saving the news for Boxing Day, so do not shriek when you hear it."

"Pooh! I never shriek."

His grin was infectious. "Very well, I shall

trust you—since I am bursting to tell someone, and there is really no one else who will appreciate it as you will. I have secured passage for my friends in Barbados."

"Oh!" cried Felicity—then clapped her hands over her mouth.

He laughed. "Mr. Ashanti's wife and daughters will be here no later than Easter."

"But that is wonderful! He will be so happy."

"It's the best gift I could give him, I fancy."

"How did you manage it?" Doubt assailed her. "Oh, Gavin—did you ask our aunt after all?"

"Devil a bit. I secured the assistance of Bishop Stanhope. He is a man of influence in such affairs. He knew of a certain missionary society—I presented my case to them—and they are gifting me the funds. I mean to pay them back as I can, but the fact that I will be unable to repay any substantial amount for some time does not worry them in the least."

"Marvelous! You do have a head on your shoulders, Gavin. I never thought of approaching the bishop. I congratulate you."

He bowed, still grinning. "Thank you. And speaking of congratulations, what of our matchmaking scheme? We can't say it before the rest of the lot, but now we're alone, we can hug ourselves, I think. I never thought matchmaking would turn out to be my forte, but I am ready to hang out my shingle and advertise for customers. Ha!"

"Yes. I forgot we planned all this." She waved a hand to indicate the house and all that was in it. "Clever of us, wasn't it? Although it may have helped, a bit, that our subjects fell head over ears in love."

Gavin looked severely at her. "I'll have you know, Felicity, that I was instrumental in bringing this about. That chuff Stanhope might have spent months desperately in love with Lulu without getting to the point." He tapped his chest and winked. "Twas I who dragged him to the finish line."

She suddenly remembered their conversation at the abbey. "Oh, of course—your brilliant secret plan. What was it?"

"Well, as he couldn't decide between Miss Bliss and Lulu, I suggested he give them a mistletoe test. This entire party was devised and planned precisely to make that happen. From what I understand, both ladies passed the test, but—ah—Lulu's score was considerably higher. So high, in fact, that Stanhope immediately offered her marriage. There, now!"

She stared blankly at him. "Score?"

"Well—I speak metaphorically, you understand. I'm sure there was no actual scorecard involved."

She pressed her fingertips against her temples. "Hold a moment. I am not following you. *What* sort of test did you suggest?"

"A mistletoe test."

"What on earth is a mistletoe test?"

Gavin laughed, pulled her quickly into his arms, and kissed her on the mouth before she knew what he was about. "That," he said.

She backed away, flustered. "Gavin, really—! Do you mean he kissed them?"

"First Almeria, then Lulu. And presto! The thing was done."

"But that is nonsensical. How could such a—a *test* —make up his mind?"

Gavin's eyebrows flew up. Then his expression turned thoughtful. "I didn't do it right," he said, shaking his head. "Come. Let me give you the kind of mistletoe test that Stanhope probably gave your sister, and you will see."

"Wh—what?"

The champagne and negus must have made her stupid. At any rate, she was slow to react when Gavin took her by the hand and pulled her into his arms, standing before the fire. Lit from below, his expression was both sardonic and tender. *Handsome,* she thought dazedly. *I could look at him forever.* She caught a whiff of Bay Rum and the clean scent of starch in his shirt. Then his mouth touched hers and the power to think abruptly left her.

His mouth was softer than expected, and surprisingly warm. His lips embraced hers, parted them, then moved, cherishing her mouth and evoking sensations she had never dreamed of. She clung to him. Melted against him. Kissed him back. Oh, heavens... this was madness. She did it anyway.

When they parted for air, she realized she had, all unconsciously, slid her arms around his neck. His were across her back and waist, and as a result they were pressed together most intimately. She was too dizzy and dazed to do anything about it, although she did recover sufficient modesty to grip his lapels rather than hug him around the neck. "Gavin," she said thickly, clinging to his coat for dear life. "There is no mistletoe."

His eyes, which had been rather glazed, focused on hers. "What?"

"There is no mistletoe here," she repeated, swaying.

He steadied her. "By Jove, you are right. We can't perform a mistletoe test without mistletoe." And with his arm still firm about her waist, he drew her to the doorway. A kissing bough hung in the arch. Mr. Stanhope had ensured that kissing boughs were in every doorway of his house, it seemed—at least on the ground floor.

They tried the mistletoe test again. At first she thought that the mistletoe made no difference—other than sanctioning what would otherwise be *most* inappropriate behavior. Then she wondered if it rather did. Something decidedly magical seemed to be happening. Then she forgot about the mistletoe entirely—and, indeed, forgot nearly everything else, swept up in the urgent, glorious madness of kissing Gavin.

What a fool she was. But no, no, she must make the most of this moment. For when would she have another chance?

Aunt Agnes's voice broke the moment like a rifle shot. "What," she barked, "is the meaning of this?"

Felicity tore her face away from his, gasped, and raised a hand to her mouth as the guilty couple fell apart. Gavin, however, continued to hold her other hand in a sustaining clasp. "Well? What does it look like, Aunt?"

He sounded perfectly composed. The wretch.

Felicity began to shake. "Champagne," she said faintly. "Negus."

Aunt Agnes frowned at her. "Are you calling for refreshment, Felicity?"

"No." She gulped. "I am saying I—I think I may have had one glass too many."

"Hum!" Aunt Agnes leaned upon her cane. Her hawk-like gaze flicked from Gavin to Felicity and back again. "And what do you have to say for yourself, you rogue?"

Gavin touched his cravat, making an infinitesimal adjustment with one finger. "Nothing, Aunt. It's Christmas Eve."

"Christmas, is it?" Her jaw worked. "And because it is Christmas Eve, you feel you may compromise my niece with impunity?"

Felicity uttered a faint cry of protest. Gavin's brows twitched together into a frown. "No such thing. I kissed her under the mistletoe, Aunt. That is all."

"I am not in my dotage," she snapped. Felicity suddenly, belatedly, saw that Aunt Agnes was not shocked at all. She was delighted, and trying to hide her delight beneath a show of bluster.

"Aunt Agnes, really!" she exclaimed. "You are roasting us. You know perfectly well that there is no harm in a mistletoe kiss."

"Mistletoe kiss, my eye," snorted Lady DuFrayne. "But if that is your story, I shall pretend to believe it."

Gavin looked slightly abashed. "In truth, I was trying to prove a point, and I'm afraid I got carried away," he said. Felicity's heart sank as he let go her hand and bowed to her. "My apologies, Cousin. I shouldn't have—er—tested you."

She drew the shreds of her tattered dignity round her and returned his bow with an inclination of her head. "Never mind, Gavin," she managed to say. "We will think no more about it."

What a liar she was. She knew she would think more about it. She tingled all over, from the top of her head to the tips of her toes. Gavin looked depressingly unaffected, however. Pride dictated that she must adopt an off-hand manner and carry on.

"Hmpf," said Aunt Agnes. "Well, come back into the library before you start a scandal." She stalked off to rejoin the party, leaving Felicity and Gavin still in the hall, standing in the arched doorway to Mr. Stanhope's parlor.

Felicity took a hasty step to one side, removing herself from the area directly beneath the kissing bough, and patted her hair self-consciously. She cleared her throat. "Well," she said. "So that is a mistletoe test. Most illuminating."

"You see how it could drive a man to make a decision."

"Yes. I daresay it could." She took a deep breath and smiled brightly. "Shall we go in?"

"If you like."

She headed for the library, but at her first step he checked her. "Felicity." She looked enquiringly at him. He gave her a devilish grin. "You passed the test."

Hot color flooded her face. "Beast! We were not to speak of it again."

"I thought you would want to know."

"Very well!" She made for the library again, and again he seized her arm.

"Having gone to the trouble of taking the test—"

She pulled her arm from his grasp. "Oh, it was no trouble," she assured him. "But it is best forgotten, I think."

"On the contrary," he said firmly. "It is best repeated."

"Repeated! No, no—"

But he had dragged her back into his arms. "Felicity Pennington," he said, with mock exasperation. "Do you push every suitor away with both hands? No wonder you are still unwed."

He tried to kiss her, but she fended him off. "You are not my suitor," she cried indignantly.

"Well, I'm dashed sure not your cousin." And his mouth came down on hers.

She clung to him for a moment only, then began to laugh. He lifted his face from hers. "Yes, vixen? I'm glad I amuse you."

"You always have."

He grinned. "Do you think you could ever love me?"

"What a question! I do love you—*Cousin.*"

"Yes, but I mean the way Lulu loves Stanhope. It gives me a pang to see their idiotish happiness. Makes me want the same thing for myself."

Felicity felt her heart leap into her throat. "With me?"

"Why not?"

Was he joking? She could not tell. Confused, she tried to laugh. "Heavens. I don't know. Ask me when I'm sober."

He looked chagrined. "But you might say no when you are sober."

She patted his arm in a consoling manner. "I am sorry, Gavin, but that is a risk you will have to take. You can't crash through life like an ox at a tea party—"

"Bull in a china shop."

She waved her hand airily. "Moose at a musicale. At any rate, you are rushing your fences, dear friend, and talking a great deal of nonsense. Now let me go. I want to return to the party."

He growled under his breath, but obeyed her. "You'll die a spinster, Felicity," he warned her.

But she felt too giddy to heed him. She had just been kissed—thoroughly kissed—by Gavin DuFrayne. Nothing, not even Gavin himself, could pull her out of the clouds. She peered slyly through her lashes at him. "Surely not," she purred. "Now that we know I can pass a mistletoe test."

*We hope you enjoyed THE MISTLETOE TEST. For more books by this author, please visit Diane Farr's website at http://www.dianefarrbooks.com*

*A bonus preview of PLAYING TO WIN follows.*

PLAYING TO WIN by Diane Farr

Chapter One

"But there is nothing to explain," said
Trevor Whitlatch. "It is quite simple, madam. You
will either compensate me for the goods you stole
eleven years ago, or you will suffer the
consequences."

A tense silence ensued, broken only by the
soft ticking of an ormolu clock on La Gianetta's
elegant mantlepiece. Mr. Whitlatch had not raised
his voice, and his smile had not wavered.
Nevertheless, Gianetta's admirably strong instinct
for self-preservation warned her that her visitor
was dangerous.

With an effort, she hid her alarm behind a
smile as smooth as Mr. Whitlatch's. Her smile
had bewitched many men over the years. She
hoped it retained enough charm to see her
through one more crisis.

On the other hand, Mr. Whitlatch was
probably young enough to be her son. Her power
to bewitch men in their prime had faded of late.
Bah! If the smile failed, she would try tears.
Surely one weapon or the other would melt the
ice glittering in Mr. Whitlatch's gaze.

She swept her graceful hands in a
dramatic, self-deprecating gesture, and addressed
Mr. Whitlatch in the throbbing tones that had
once held audiences spellbound. "Ah, *m'sieur,*
you must understand! The world was a different

place in 1791, was it not? I was so bewildered, so frightened—all of France in such turmoil! I was leaving my home, all my possessions behind. My life was in ruins. I hardly knew what I did. I never meant to take the rubies off your ship, *m'sieur;* it was a mistake."

"Yes, it was," he agreed. "A serious mistake." Mr. Whitlatch's swarthiness gave his grin the swift, white flash of a tiger's snarl.

He leaned back in the fragile, spindle-legged chair, jammed his hands in his pockets and stretched his long, booted legs across her Aubusson carpet. The effect of this rudeness was that La Gianetta's elegant receiving room seemed suddenly small and stuffy. Trevor Whitlatch was a large man. He inhabited an impressive physique, and several years at sea and abroad had darkened his already harsh features. This, together with the careless way he shrugged into his clothes, gave him an out-of-doors air that dwarfed most interiors. Gianetta fervently hoped her delicate furniture would hold him. She could ill afford to replace it.

Mr. Whitlatch's unexpected demand could not have come at a more unfortunate time. She was bitterly aware that her desirability increasingly depended upon illusion. She still possessed her hypnotic, lightly-accented voice and remnants of the exotic beauty that had made her famous, but she knew that her prominence among London's demimonde was due more to her celebrated name, and the style in which she lived, than what remained of her personal attractions. If her creditors began to suspect how perilously close to bankruptcy she was, they would hound her into debtors' prison.

She schooled her features into a look of gentle inquiry. "May I ask what makes the collection of this old debt suddenly a matter of importance? I thought, naturally, that you forgave my little misstep. A small thing to miss, among the riches you bore on that ship alone—and you with so many more ships, so many more voyages! I daresay you would have given me the rubies, had I asked for them. Such a generous young man you were! And I so destitute! I believed if you noticed the loss at all, you considered it a charity, *m'sieur.*"

His smile turned sardonic. "I prefer to choose my charities, madam, not have them forced upon me by theft."

"Then why did you not demand the jewels' return immediately? I have heard nothing from you for eleven years. Can you blame me for thinking you considered the rubies a gift?"

"Yes, I can blame you," he said affably. "I do blame you. I thought I made that clear."

"Ah, yes, today! But then? Then, *m'sieur?* I would have returned them to you at once, I swear!" La Gianetta made play with a fine pair of eyes.

Mr. Whitlatch was unmoved. "Return them to me now," he offered.

She spread her hands helplessly. "Now? I do not keep them in my house, *m'sieur.*"

"No, you don't," he agreed blandly. "Because you sold the rubies immediately upon your arrival in England."

Gianetta's eyes flashed defiance. *"Alors!* Do you mock me? Yes, I sold them. Why fly from death in France, only to starve in England?"

Mr. Whitlatch's lip curled. "You could have sold in London what you had sold for years in Paris. Englishmen pay just as handsomely as Frenchmen for it. I suppose you have learned that by now."

She arched one delicately drawn eyebrow. Her voice dripped honey. *"M'sieur* flatters me! But if you know I do not have the rubies, why are you here? Is it possible you have suffered some reversal, sir, that makes it necessary for you to recover funds—even from such as I?"

Mr. Whitlatch uttered a short bark of laughter. "Unlikely!" he remarked. "No, ma'am, I am here only because your conduct has brought you to my notice once again. Can you guess how?"

She shook her head, but regarded him warily from beneath her lashes.

"No? I will tell you." But a small silence fell as Mr. Whitlatch pressed the tips of his long fingers together and frowned, unseeing, at the carpet. When he finally began speaking, his gaze returned to La Gianetta's face and watched her keenly.

"When you repaid my kindness with theft eleven years ago, I let it go. Your conduct was disgusting, but I did not propose to make myself a laughingstock by prosecuting you. You had played me for a fool. You knew it, and I knew it. I saw no need for the world to know it. So I swallowed my pride and chalked the episode up to experience. You had crossed me, but only once." His voice became silky, and Gianetta shivered. "No one, male or female, crosses Trevor Whitlatch twice."

"Twice? But I have done nothing else to you!"

"No, not to me." His eyes lit with sardonic amusement. "Never to me, in point of fact. Even the rubies were not stolen from me. Everything on that ship belonged to my uncle. In those days, I acted merely as his agent, bringing his goods safely from India to England."

She pounced on this digression. "If that is so, you do wrong to blame me. The fault is entirely your own! Your impulse to save my life

200

was admirable, but you should not have followed it." Her hands swept dramatically to her temples. "You should have left me in Marseilles, to die at the hands of that mob!"

"I was extremely young, and—er—impressionable." Mr. Whitlatch's teeth flashed in another swift grin. "You were really very lovely."

She inclined her head stiffly, reluctantly acknowledging the compliment. His eyes twinkled. "You are still easy on the eyes, Gianetta. But in 1791 you were Beauty itself, to a boy who had been at sea entirely too long. And to have so famous a creature as La Gianetta begging for my help—to have stumbled upon Beauty in Distress, and have the means of rescuing her! Who could resist? Not I! That is why I promptly threw caution to the winds, concealed you on my uncle's ship, and brought you safely out of France to England with all the speed I could muster."

"Your conduct was noble, *m'sieur*. Noble! I have ever said so. I was deeply grateful to you."

Mr. Whitlatch's gaze hardened. "So grateful, in fact, that you stole a chest of jewels from your benefactor."

"But, no—a small box!" she demurred, clasping one white hand to her bosom in a gesture eloquent of pained protest.

"A small box of extremely valuable stones. You knew the theft would go undetected until the inventory sheets were checked, by which time you had disappeared. I was young, with a young man's vanity; you gambled that I would rather make up the difference out of my own pocket than publish to the world how La Gianetta had used me. It was a cynical gamble on your part, madam, but you won it. You then sold the stones and used the money to establish yourself here. You were quite brazen about it. You made no attempt to hide your identity."

La Gianetta's expressive eyes were raised to his face. "My identity is my fortune, Mr. Whitlatch."

"I daresay," he said drily. "And now that famous name of yours is lending its *cachet* to another enterprise that seems quite profitable. You run an elegant, and very popular, gaming hell."

A demure smile curved her lips. "I hold a few private card parties, *m'sieur.*"

"Is that the euphemism you prefer? Very well. Your private card parties are extremely well attended, are they not? I understand the attraction of your rooms is enhanced by the presence of certain young women. One hears that these women are every bit as alluring as they are—accommodating."

La Gianetta waved a dismissive hand. "People will say anything," she cooed. "Naturally I employ certain girls to run the faro table, the roulette wheel—"

Mr. Whitlatch sat upright, feigning surprise. "Faro and roulette? At a private card party?"

She stiffened, then eyed him with acute dislike. "As you say, *m'sieur*. I misspoke."

"Hm. Well, let that pass. At any rate, we now come to the point where your activities crossed me a second time."

"Crossed you! How?"

Mr. Whitlatch leaned forward menacingly. "You have in your employ a certain female who, I have reason to believe, makes it her business to prey upon gullible young men."

As this description could be applied to any of the young women presently in her employ, La Gianetta lifted an eyebrow but remained silent.

"This creature has done irreparable harm

to a young friend of mine. My friend, in telling me his tale, extracted a promise from me. I promised that I would take no vengeance upon the girl. My hands are tied, then, as far as punishing the hussy who is the principal actor in this little drama. However, madam, I have no doubt that the notorious La Gianetta, though not appearing on the stage, directed the play."

La Gianetta, now thoroughly alarmed, hid behind a screen of indignation. "I do not know what you mean. What has happened? How am I to blame? Ah, *dieu!* I do not understand any of it!"

"Again I say, the matter is simple. I promised my friend that I would not approach your hireling. I therefore approach you." He leaned back in the fragile chair, regarding her keenly. "Your recent crime against my friend I am not at liberty to avenge. I therefore will avenge your past crime against myself—which I otherwise might never have done. Ironic, is it not? But there it is. 'The mills of God grind slowly, yet they grind exceeding small.' You may not understand the literary allusion, but I am sure you understand the rest of it well enough."

La Gianetta nervously fingered the pearls clasped round her throat. For a moment she wondered if she could offer them to Mr. Whitlatch in lieu of the rubies. How long would it be before he discovered the pearls were paste? Not long, she decided. Mr. Whitlatch was no fool.

"What do you want?" she whispered. "You are a businessman, Mr. Whitlatch. There is no profit to you in sending me to prison. What can I offer you to make amends?"

"Nothing less than the value of the rubies, as listed on my uncle's inventory sheet in 1791. And be grateful I do not charge you interest."

"What is the sum?"

He named it. La Gianetta paled beneath

her rouge. She had sold the gems for a fraction of their value, and still they had brought her enough to establish herself in style. She had no hope of paying him back the amount she had originally received for the jewels, let alone their actual worth. Ruin stared her in the face.

"I cannot possibly raise such a sum today. You must give me time," she said hoarsely.

"But you will pay it?"

"Yes, yes, of course I will pay it!"

Mr. Whitlatch studied her for a moment. Her eyes dropped beneath his level gaze. "Spoken too easily, Gianetta. Exactly how do you propose to pay me?"

"How? Why, I will sell something, of course."

"What will you sell?" he inquired softly.

La Gianetta lifted one white shoulder in a petulant shrug. "That is no concern of yours."

"Forgive me, but I think it is." His eyes bored into her. "In fact, I think it might be foolish for me to leave empty-handed this morning. Who knows? You might find yourself suddenly called out of town. And then where would I be? Particularly if you failed to return." He chuckled at the glare of pure hatred she shot him. "Exactly so, ma'am! I would be wise to take away with me whatever item you possess that you think might fetch such a price."

The clock ticked. Motes of dust danced in the thin November sunlight pouring through the window. La Gianetta was clearly at a loss. Mr. Whitlatch waited politely.

Slowly her look of confusion was replaced by an arrested look; she grew thoughtful. She cast him a speculative glance. He raised an eyebrow inquiringly. That somehow seemed to decide her. She reached out briskly and rang for a servant.

"I will show you my most valuable possession," she told him composedly. "You will decide its worth for yourself."

Mr. Whitlatch was conscious of a feeling of surprise. What the devil was she about? He had expected tears, begging, panic. Instead, La Gianetta looked like a cat at a creampot. She almost purred.

He frowned. "I am not competent to judge the value of jewelry on sight. If you propose to send me away with some trumpery bestowed on you by—"

He broke off, instantly suspicious. Gianetta's shoulders were shaking with silent laughter.

"You are competent to judge the value of this particular jewel, Mr. Whitlatch. All the world knows you are something of a connoisseur in this line."

A scrawny wench in a mob cap arrived, and La Gianetta entered into a soft-voiced colloquy in French. Mystified, Mr. Whitlatch watched as the servant uttered a frightened protest, which Gianetta swiftly quelled with a sharp word. The girl then withdrew, eyes big with alarm, to perform whatever office her mistress had requested.

"Marie is reluctant to do my bidding, Mr. Whitlatch. You have seen her reluctance." La Gianetta's eyes blinked rapidly, but Mr. Whitlatch perceived that the eyes behind the fluttering lashes were dry. "Ah, *m'sieur,* if you only knew what this costs me! I, too, am reluctant to bring before you my precious jewel, my pearl of great price. I very much fear that you will take my treasure away with you, never again to be seen by me! But I will not blame you; no, for this prize has only to be seen to be desired. You will be amazed, Mr. Whitlatch. Very few people know of my treasure's existence. My treasure of incalculable worth!"

Mr. Whitlatch's eyes narrowed. Gianetta sounded exactly like a Calcutta street peddlar who had once tried to sell him a brass ornament, swearing it was gold. "What sort of treasure, madam?"

She again made play with her eyelashes. "My only child, sir. A daughter."

With an oath, Mr. Whitlatch rose and strode to the window. "I am no slaver, madam! You may keep your daughter."

Her smile reflected in the windowpane. "You have not seen her yet," she said simply.

Mr. Whitlatch, torn between exasperation and curiosity, turned his scowling gaze back to his hostess. "I never heard that you had a daughter."

The catlike smile still curved her painted mouth. "Few know of her existence, and no one has seen her." La Gianetta's voice resumed its dramatic throb. "She is completely untouched, sir."

Mr. Whitlatch gave an inelegant snort. A likely tale! He was about to be presented with some pretty child La Gianetta had picked up, God knows where, planning to foist upon the public as her own. Rich men would vie for the privilege of deflowering any wench believed to be the daughter of the legendary Gianetta. The chit would fetch a high price. He supposed his demand for payment had upset these well-laid plans, and Gianetta now would try to fob him off with the girl instead of proper repayment. Mr. Whitlatch felt a stab of disgust. La Gianetta was a whore to her very soul.

"Let me be sure I understand you, madam. Do you propose to give me this unfortunate female in exchange for my stolen property? You would not hesitate to sell your 'daughter' to a virtual stranger?"

"You are no stranger to me, Mr. Whitlatch. It is true we did not know one another before you rescued me from France, and we have not seen each other since, but your conduct in 1791 was heroic. Heroic! There is no other word for it."

He almost yelped with derision. "I can think of several other words for it!"

She waved this aside. "Your reputation, too, is well known to me. You are an honorable man, just and fair in all your dealings."

A self-mocking grin flashed across his features. "If you believe me to be honorable where women are concerned, madam, you have been strangely misinformed."

To his surprise, La Gianetta met his eyes frankly for the first time. "You are mistaken, Mr. Whitlatch. You offer marriage to no one, so you believe yourself to be a hardened rake. But me, I have some experience of rakes, *m'sieur!* You are no rake. On the contrary; you are a romantic."

"I?" gasped Mr. Whitlatch, revolted.

She smiled serenely. "You have told me, *m'sieur,* that you found me beautiful eleven years ago. I was completely in your power for many days, and deeply grateful to you as well. I would have refused you nothing. You must have known this, yet you never touched me."

Mr. Whitlatch's frown returned. He shrugged, and leaned negligently against the window. "Only a cad would take advantage of a woman in such circumstances."

"My point precisely, sir. You are no cad. You would not take unfair advantage of a woman—even such a woman as La Gianetta." A bitter chuckle shook her. "Only a true romantic refuses to dishonor a harlot! My Clarissa, if she pleases you, will be fairly treated."

"Thank you, but I have no interest in your Clarissa! Touched or untouched, seen or unseen, your daughter or someone else's, there is not a female on the planet as valuable as those rubies."

La Gianetta laughed out loud at this. "Again your reputation belies you! I am sure you have spent far more than that, on any one of the incognitas you have had in your keeping. The rubies were nothing, less than nothing, compared to a certain set of diamonds—"

"Yes, well, never mind that!" interrupted Mr. Whitlatch, impatiently jamming his hands into his pockets. "Never was money more ill-spent! I have no desire to repeat such folly. I'll be the first to admit I have a soft spot for a pretty face, but at the moment I am not in the market for—"

He broke off as the door opened. A girl in a pale blue gown entered noiselessly and stood beside Gianetta's chair. Mr. Whitlatch stared. His hands, as if moving of their own volition, removed themselves from his pockets and his careless slouch slowly straightened.

His first thought was that he had seldom, if ever, beheld such beauty in human form. His second was that it was extremely clever of La Gianetta to dress the girl so chastely. Her loveliness was enhanced by the simplicity of her frock, the modesty of the high neckline and absence of frills. But this girl would be beautiful if she were wrapped in burlap, he realized. She had the unconscious, feral grace of a deer. And her features! Flawless.

Was it possible this girl was actually La Gianetta's daughter? He could not help hoping that she was. It would be a great thing, after all, to banish his earlier picture of an innocent maiden stolen from some peasant family. It would be a great thing, in fact, to forget he ever supposed this girl could be innocent. If she was truly La Gianetta's daughter, one could then entertain the thought—merely the thought, mind you—of accepting this preposterous offer.

It was possible to trace a resemblance. She had the raven's-wing hair, the soft mouth and straight little nose. She also had a radiant, soft, pink-and-white complexion; the very look that La Gianetta aped with cosmetics. It was all the more dramatic against the darkness of the girl's hair and eyes. Or were her eyes dark?

As if hearing his thought, she suddenly raised her eyes to his and he was dazzled. Framed by black lashes, her eyes were a bright, cerulean blue; a blue usually reserved by the Maker for the eyes of infants and angels.

His decision was made too swiftly for Reason to intervene. Oh, yes, he had a soft spot for a pretty face. And a face like this one could bring him to the point of idiocy. He knew this about himself; he was resigned. La Gianetta had judged her man well.

He would give anything, anything at all, to possess this piece of perfection.

Mr. Whitlatch sighed, and flung up a hand in surrender. "Very well, madam. Very well."

La Gianetta's eyes snapped eagerly. "You will consider my debt paid in full, Mr. Whitlatch?"

"Completely."

"Bien! Clarissa, my love, ask Marie to pack up your things. You will be taking a little journey, I think."

Mr. Whitlatch was too bemused to notice the nervousness with which Gianetta uttered these words; nor the gesture, half supplication, half warning, that went with them. Rapt in his contemplation of Clarissa's beauty, he saw only her graceful, submissive curtsey before she exited. He entirely missed the murderous fury in the glance she threw La Gianetta as the door closed.

Her mother's servant, with profuse apologies, was locking her in the garret again. Listening to the tumblers turning in the lock as Marie fumbled nervously with the key, Clarissa leaned against the closed door and tried to regain her composure. She was trembling with anger.

So she would be taking a 'little journey,' would she? In the company of that man, no doubt. Outrageous! Disgraceful! That any mother could make such an arrangement for her own daughter was incredible. But Clarissa had seen enough of her mother, and her mother's household, in the last two days to believe anything.

She closed her eyes, and furious tears stung the back of her eyelids. Since the moment of her arrival, she had vowed to escape this den of iniquity as soon as ever she could. And after she had refused to fall in with her mother's original plans for her, she had spent the past two days locked in this makeshift bedchamber. There had been plenty of time to think, and plan, and find a way out of this intolerable situation. Only no plan had occurred to her.

She had no one to turn to. No friends, no family. All the money she had in the world was knotted in a handkerchief in the bottom of her reticule. After the expense of traveling to London from the Bathurst Ladies' Academy, her resources amounted to less than seventeen guineas.

She had paced this room for many of the past forty-eight hours, vainly wracking her brain to think of a way out. How could she support herself? How could she avoid the life of debauchery her mother was so eager to thrust upon her? Her situation seemed hopeless indeed. And now this man, this stranger, had appeared out of nowhere to take her away.

Doubtless it was another scheme of Gianetta's to force her unwilling daughter into her own footsteps. But perhaps Clarissa could find a way to foil her mother's plans. Perhaps the man could be reasoned with. He might even take pity on her plight. And even if he did not, surely she could find a way of escape—if only she could get out from under this roof!

Besides, there was always a chance that his intentions were perfectly honorable. She knew nothing about this man, or what he wanted. Why should she suppose the worst? For that matter, she knew very little about her mother. It was possible that Clarissa's pleas and protestations— although they had seemed to have no impact whatsoever at the time—had prevailed, once Mother had had a chance to reflect upon them. Perhaps La Gianetta had struck a bargain with this man to offer her daughter respectable employment. Anything was possible.

"And anything would be preferable to staying here—anything at all!" she whispered. Clarissa took a deep breath, opened her eyes, and resolutely began to pack.

This task did not take long. Her possessions were few, and since from the day she arrived she had desired nothing more than to depart, she had never fully unpacked her trunk. Her throat ached with unshed tears as she gathered her precious trinkets. Here was the pewter thimble Jane Peele had given her, to remember her by. And here, the farewell letter the six youngest schoolgirls had signed. She fought the memories back. She must not think of it. It did no good to think of it.

She was standing before a cracked pier glass, buttoning her redingote, when a timid knock sounded. Marie's muffled voice wafted through the keyhole.

"Mademoiselle? You wish for help with ze packing?"

"No, thank you. I am quite finished," replied Clarissa. A soft exclamation and the rattling of the key heralded the entrance of poor Marie, who sidled nervously in as if expecting to be slapped. Their eyes met in the glass, and Clarissa smiled reassuringly.

"You see?" she said, waving a hand to indicate the single trunk and two bandboxes. "That is everything."

Marie blinked. It was evident that Clarissa's past conduct had led Marie to expect fierce resistance, not this calm complaisance. In proof of this, two burly individuals now stepped through the door. Marie had brought reinforcements. One of the men Clarissa recognized as her mother's footman, but the other appeared to be a hired porter.

"Very good, mademoiselle," stammered Marie. She nodded at the men, and each took a bandbox and one end of the trunk. As they lumbered off, Marie edged toward the door.

"One moment, please!" said Clarissa, turning to face the little servant. Marie gulped, and shrank back toward the wall.

"For heaven's sake, I am not going to hurt you! I only want to know the name of the man downstairs. Do you know his name?"

Marie stared. "But, Mademoiselle, he is *Trevor Whitlatch!*" she breathed ecstatically.

The name meant nothing to Clarissa. She frowned. "Whitlatch? The Devonshire family?"

Marie shook her head vehemently. "I do

not know, Mademoiselle, but ze Monsieur Whitlatch, he is a man *très distingué!*"

Clarissa raised an eyebrow. "Famous, is he? For what?"

Marie clasped her hands at her thin bosom and broke into an enthusiastic, and extremely idiomatic, stream of French. Clarissa was only able to decipher about every third word, and finally interrupted her. "Thank you, Marie, but I cannot follow what you are saying! Something about India, and ships. Are you telling me this man Whitlatch is a nabob?"

"Nay-bob? I do not know zis word, Mademoiselle. But you understand ze man is rich, yes? Ver-r-r-ry rich! You will live like ze queen, *hein?*" She rolled her eyes expressively, beaming at Clarissa.

Clarissa's veins turned to ice, and her hands clenched involuntarily. "Dear God," she whispered. "Then it is as I feared."

Marie wrinkled her nose. "Please?"

Clarissa took a deep breath. "Marie, you must tell me what you know about this man, and *why* he is taking me away." She saw the alarm return to Marie's features, and smiled encouragingly. "Come, I won't blame you! I know you are only the messenger."

Marie gulped, and began twisting her apron. "Oh, mademoiselle, I do not know all, me! But Monsieur Whitlatch, today he is having ze *contretemps* with Madame, *non?* And Madame, she gives him you. Now he is happy, and ze *contretemps,* it is at an end."

Clarissa's eyes widened in horror. "She *gave* me to him? To end a dispute?"

Marie nodded vigorously. "But yes!" she said, with a sigh of envy. "You will go with him, and you will live like ze queen!" She then bobbed a quick curtsey, and slipped out the door.

Marie's air of eager congratulation was the most shocking thing of all. How could anyone find such a bargain anything but reprehensible? Fear stole along her nerves. Given to the man! Heaven defend her! All her life she had tried to live respectably, had tried to banish all traces of her mother's influence, had tried to deny, by the sheer force of her own virtue, whose daughter she was—only to fall into her mother's clutches and be ruined! Oh, it was dreadful! She dared not think what the stranger might require of her.

Four years ago, when she was sixteen, the music master had tried to kiss her. Miss Bathurst had been very angry—bless her!—and the music master had lost his situation. But Clarissa remembered the scene all too clearly. It had been most unpleasant. And now this man, this Trevor Whitlatch, would doubtless try the same thing. Men enjoyed taking such liberties, one was told. She had even heard other girls at the Academy whisper that kisses were only the beginning of what a man could do to a girl. She had heard there were other, more dreadful, intimacies than the pressing together of two mouths. But Clarissa's imagination failed her when she tried to think beyond kisses. A kiss, in her experience, was invasion enough. She shuddered.

Well. There was no help for it. She could not stay locked in her mother's attic forever. A dangerous path of escape was set before her, but she would take it. At least until another path presented itself. And whatever happened, she vowed, she would never return to this house.

She firmly tied the strings of her best bonnet beneath her chin. It had a deep poke front, so if Mr. Whitlatch had any immediate intention of kissing her it would be difficult for him to execute his plan. She began to pull on her gloves, then hesitated.

Mr. Whitlatch had appeared to be a man of some strength.

Tossing the gloves aside, she rummaged hastily through a drawer and, with a triumphant little smile, unearthed a long and wicked-looking hat pin. Standing before the mirror, she pushed the hat pin carefully through the wide satin ribbon on the top of her bonnet. She patted it to reassure herself of its exact location.

*"En garde, Monsieur!"* Clarissa whispered to her reflection. Then she picked up her gloves and walked downstairs.

*We hope you enjoyed this preview of PLAYING TO WIN. For more books by this author, please visit Diane Farr's website at http://www.dianefarrbooks.com*

Diane Farr was first published at the age of eight when the local newspaper printed one of her poems. She has spent most of her life with her nose in a book — sometimes reading, sometimes writing. Eventually she produced eight historical romances and a novella, all published by Signet Books. She is also the author of an award-winning teen paranormal series: *The Spellspinners*. Diane lives in Northern California with two cats and a husband. You can learn more about her books at dianefarrbooks.com.